ROPES

BURNING SAINTS MC BOOK #3

JACK DAVENPORT

2020 Jack Davenport
Copyright © 2018, 2020 Trixie Publishing, Inc.
All rights reserved.
Published in the United States

Ropes is a work of fiction. Names, characters, places, and incidents are the products of the author's imagination and are used fictitiously. Any resemblance to actual events, locales, or persons, living or dead, is entirely coincidental.

Cover Art
Jack Davenport

TRIXIE
PUBLISHING

ISBN: 9798617761421

Printed in the USA
All Rights Reserved

Oh, good gravy, this book is good. And I'm not just saying that because he does other amazing things with his fingers!

~ Piper Davenport, Contemporary Romance Author

Liz Kelly
Your insights are amazing and always spot on. Thank you!

Piper
I couldn't do any of this without you. Literally, my fingers would fall off and I'd be a vegetable.

Brandy G.
Thank you for the million reads and your attention to detail!!! You're amazing.

Gail G.
You're a rock star! Thank you for all your help!

Mary H.
A million thanks! You're an angel.

For Harper & Felicia

It's such a blast sailing these crazy seas with y'all.

For "Father" Justin

To the greatest emcee in international waters. Keep the pack poppin'!

For my fellow Book Splashers

*I look forward to EVERY sailing with you!!!
You are amazing!*

ONE

BURNING SAINTS

Ropes

"**O**H MY GOD, *baby, don't stop," she said as I slammed into her again and again. "I'm going to come," she cried as I felt the sting of her fingernails clawing their way down my back.*

"Not until I say," I commanded and pulled out entirely, causing her to writhe in delicious agony.

"Not fair," she said on a gasp. "Please… fuck me. Please, fuck me now."

"On your knees," I commanded, and she did as she was told. I loved her in this position, as it gave me the most access to her entire body. I fisted my rigid cock and slammed back into her pussy without warning, feeling her walls contract around me as her cum soaked my dick. I smacked her ass for her disobedience, but it only made her come harder.

"I told you there would be consequences for coming without me, and now you're going to have to pay for breaking the rules," I said, rising to my feet.

She was still on her hands and knees, her glorious ass sticking up in the air. I had so many things planned for that ass. I was almost glad I hadn't come yet.

"Yes please. Please... make me pay," she said, still out of breath, in a voice that somehow managed to make me even harder than I was.

"You'd be wise to not write checks your ass can't cover," I warned as I walked across the room toward my steamer trunk.

"You don't scare me," Cherry said with a giggle, as she sat up. Her beautiful red curls hung down, barely able to cover her perfect breasts. Fucking a woman with natural tits was more of a turn-on than I could have imagined.

"My goal isn't to scare you," I said, unlocking the trunk. "It's to teach you, and I'm afraid today's lesson might hurt a little."

I pulled out a long wooden paddle from the trunk, her eyes widened, and she let out a slight gasp.

The heavy oak door to Minus's office swung open wildly, crashing against the wall with a thud. I slammed my laptop closed and hoped the auto-save function had done its job properly. Despite the noise around the Sanctuary, the half hour I'd spent outside Minus's office had served as productive writing time. I'd managed to write most of a scene and the tightness in my jeans told me it was a good one.

"Fuckin' Portland hippie bureaucrats and their goddamned permits!" Minus bellowed from the doorway before turning his attention to me. "Hey, Ropes. Come on in, sorry to keep you waiting," he said, his usual boyish smile returning instantly. "I was stuck on a call," he continued, as he stepped aside. "The city is giving us shit about missing permits at one of our build sites. Something about our organic recycling needing to be gluten free or some horse shit."

Our club was currently going through several major construction builds, all in the name of 'progress and change.'

"No problem," I said as I slipped my laptop into my satchel, which I slung in front of me, attempting to hide the semi-chub I was sporting.

"Nice purse," Minus said as I passed him in the doorway.

I raised an eyebrow. "What? Clutch gives you shit about your pretty cowboy boots, so you've gotta bust my balls about my satchel?"

"Call it what you want, but that's a fuckin' purse," he replied as we made our way inside and he closed the door. There weren't many brothers hanging around the Sanctuary today, but Minus was a private guy.

"I use it to carry my laptop," I said.

"Yeah, well some people use laptop cases or backpacks, so forgive me if I'm slow to accept that thing as anything other than a fashion accessory."

"Am I stealin' your thunder, Hop Along?"

"Is that all you got? More lame-ass cowboy jokes?" Minus protested. "You assholes still haven't gotten this shit out your system yet? I've been back from Savannah long enough don'tcha think?"

"Not long enough to get overhearing you talk like a good ol' boy," I replied.

"Shit, you can drive east for a couple hours and run into as many rednecks as I ever did in Georgia," Minus said.

"But none with boots as *puuurdy* as yours," I said.

"Don't worry, buddy, I think your status as best-dressed member of the club is still safe for the time being," Minus replied.

"Forget your boots. I'm still trying to wrap my mind around you on a horse," I said.

He smiled wide "Shit, man, once you get movin' on a horse, a bike starts to feel kinda tame."

Minus had only been the Burning Saints president for a short time, but our friendship had cemented itself years ago. He and his best friend, Clutch, threw in with the club as prospects a couple of years before my brother, Sweet Pea, and me. Soon, the four of us, along with another prospect named

3

Grover, had become a solid crew and were eventually all patched-in together.

Now, almost a decade later, Minus was the club's president, Clutch was the Sergeant at Arms, and Grover was laying in an unmarked grave somewhere in Mexico. Funny how things work out. As for me and Pea, we're still loyal soldiers. Street level guys. Not officers, but high ranking and well-respected, which was just fine by me. I had a life outside the club and had zero desire to climb the ranks. My little brother, on the other hand, had bigger plans for himself within the club, but I tried my best to stay out of his business and let him cut his own trail.

"You finishing a presentation out there or something?" Minus asked, as we took our seats, him behind Cutter's old desk, and me on the well-worn leather sofa that, as far as I could tell, had been here since dinosaurs roamed the Pacific Northwest.

"What? No... well, sort of, I guess. Not really," I said nervously, glancing down at the well-worn leather bag.

"Relax, man. What the fuck are you so jumpy about?" Minus asked, picking up on my nervous energy.

"This is just really fuckin' weird," I admitted, looking around the office.

"What? Me being the president, or the club going straight?"

"Both," I said with a laugh. "Plus, being here in Cutter's old office."

"Tell *me* about it," he said, raising an eyebrow.

The sudden and tragic loss of the Burning Saints' founder and president, Cutter, had dealt a major blow to the entire club. His firm but fair approach had made him a popular leader and a respected man. More importantly, his legendary reputation as a ruthless businessman made him feared on the street. That was paramount to the club's survival, as our stock in trade was protection. We kept gangs and other criminal organizations off the backs of business owners wherever we had a local chapter. We collected a fair monthly fee for our services and would often invest in businesses as well if

Cutter saw potential. Over time, the club had developed long-lasting relationships with business owners all over Portland that would serve us well over the years.

Around the time of Cutter's death, the club was given two major pieces of news. First, that Minus, despite his relatively young age and lack of ranking, would become the club's next president, and secondly, that the Burning Saints, a notorious gang of outlaw bikers, would only be operating legal, legitimate businesses from this point forward. This included putting a halt on all current street level operations immediately.

These controversial, and financially monumental, decisions made by Cutter himself had caused division within the club, but Minus was determined to see Cutter's final wishes granted. I was here today because of a mandate that he'd given all members, find new and legal ways for the club to earn money and present the ideas to him as soon as possible. Minus wanted us using our minds instead of our fists, and he expected full compliance.

"You're a smart guy and I have no doubt that you'll have some good business ideas," he said, smiling warmly. Minus was as tough as nails and built like a brick shithouse, but he had a way of making people feel at ease and relaxed. Over the years, some people would mistake his calm and casual demeanor for weakness, but they'd never make that same mistake twice. I thought Minus had the makings of a great president, but that opinion wasn't shared by everyone, including my brother and our road captain, Wolf.

"Look, man," I said sheepishly. "Honestly, I only have one idea and I'm not sure how you're going to react to it."

"As long as it's not another goddamned strip club, you should be fine," he said with a groan. "The last three guys all promised something fresh, but in the end, it was poles, bad hot wings, and glitter covered titties."

"I can guarantee my plan is *not* to open a strip club," I replied.

"Well, then, lay it on me," he said, extending his arms wide open.

I swallowed and took a deep breath.

"I've been writing and self-publishing erotic romance novels for the past three years. I'm starting to make surprisingly good money at it and think I could expand my business in a way that could generate some revenue for the club. In order to increase my visibility and profitability within the marketplace, I'm going to need to start going to book signings and author events."

Minus's smile dropped completely, and his outstretched arms hit the table with a sickening thud. "You've gotta be shitting me."

* * *

Devlin

Sally Anne's was packed, even for a Saturday night. From what I'd gathered since punching in, we seemed to have an influx of new faces. The place was only scarcely populated with the usual assortment of bikers and boozers, and instead was primarily occupied by portly, middle-aged guys in superhero t-shirts and cargo shorts.

"Be careful out there, sweetie. There's some sort of asshole convention in town or something," Sally Anne called out from the bar, where a few of the younger members of the Burning Saints MC were sitting. The club were part owners in Sally Anne's place, making its members regular fixtures around here. They were good to have around for security purposes, although it didn't look like tonight's crowd posed much of a threat.

I finished tying my apron and made my way into the sea of humanity that was this evening's dinner crowd. Waitressing at Sally Anne's was supposed to be a part-time, temporary solution to my lack of cash flow, but had become a full-time job. In all honesty, this was the last thing I wanted to be doing, but I needed the money and high paying jobs in Portland were scarce for anyone who didn't want to work in an office, which I most certainly did not.

My real dream was to be a full-time tattoo artist, with a

place of my own. I had recently started working as a free-lance artist at a couple of local shops, so I could keep my chops up while building my clientele, but the work wasn't regular enough. I needed my own shop, thus the nightly grind at what was essentially a biker bar. When I wasn't spilling beer here or hustling for tattoo appointments I was sketching or painting. Trying my best to push my boundaries as an artist.

"Hi there, welcome to Sally Anne's, my name is Devlin. What can I get you?" I asked the trio of doughy men seated before me. The words flowed from my mouth in an all-too familiar rhythm and cadence that made me uneasy. I could not allow myself to get comfortable in this job.

"Water's just fine," one of the men replied, without making eye contact.

"Okay, water to drink for you sir. How about you guys? What can I get you from the bar?" I asked the other two men in a cheery tone.

"Water only for all of us," the first man said.

"Just w… water?" I asked, unable to hide my shock. The place is packed, and these jackasses were taking up an entire table to sit and drink fucking *water*?

"We're just here for the Magic Lady," the second schlub piped up, distractedly looking to the opposite corner of the room near the restrooms and Portland's last functioning pay phone.

"The who?" I asked, totally unaware of who they were talking about. If Sally Anne had booked a magic act, this was the first I was hearing of it, but it would explain the plague of nerds that had descended upon the place.

"The Magic Lady! I still can't believe that you guys have one!" he replied in a tone that almost registered as excited.

"And that you actually let people play her," the third guy chimed in.

"I'm sorry. My shift just started, and I think I may have missed something. Who is the Magic Lady?"

The "Three Nerdmigos" looked up at me like I'd just taken a dump on their table.

7

"The Zidware Pinball USA Magic Lady. The one you have over there," nerd number one, said pointing furiously.

I shrugged, not knowing at all what he was talking about. Sally Anne's had a few old video games in a corner near the pool tables, but I'd never paid any attention to them. From what I could recall there was only one regular that ever paid any attention to the game area at all.

"The Magic Lady? Designed by John Popadiuk?" he asked, his voice rising in pitch with each question.

"Sorry guys. I have no idea what you're talking about, but if you aren't drinking then I've gotta go take some orders from other tables, okay?" I said, toning my niceties down a few notches. These clowns didn't look like the tipping type anyway.

"You'll find most of the group will be drinking club soda or water tonight," he said, still transfixed on the flurry of activity in the corner.

"Group?" I asked, my irritation level starting to rise.

"The P.S.S.P.E.," he said plainly.

"The what?"

"The Portland Society of Sober Pinball Enthusiasts," he replied, finally making eye contact, which I immediately wished he hadn't.

"That's not a thing," I blurted out.

The alpha nerd rose to his feet. "It most certainly is. We are a sanctioned member of the Nation Pinball Association of America and our chapter president always carries the certificate with him, as is required by the society's bylaws.

"Are you the club's president?" I asked.

"I am not, as I was unsuccessful in securing the winning number of votes during this past election," he said, quickly returning to his seat.

"I'm sorry to hear that, but I…"

"Our president's name is Troy Holden and you'll likely find him hogging the Magic Lady the entire evening," he said, pouting.

"Riiiight. And none of you guys in here tonight are drinking?" I asked, motioning to the crowd.

8

"We're all straight edge," Nerd Two said.

"Shut up, Randy," the Alpha Nerd barked before turning back to me. "We're just here for the Magic Lady."

"Which is some sort of *pinball machine*?" I asked.

"Not just any pinball machine," he huffed. "There were only nineteen made. It took six years and over a million dollars to design," he said as if Sally Anne's had a Rembrandt hanging on the wall that I'd mistaken for "Dogs Playing Poker."

"Okay, great. Thanks for the info, I think I hear my boss calling me," I said, and made a beeline for the bar. I had a feeling Sally Anne was going to be none too pleased with the news that her bar was currently filled with a bunch of teetotalers. I'd only encountered one table full of these guys and I was already done. I could handle drunk bikers all night long, but these assholes had to go. Not to mention, who still played pinball, or would plan an entire night around gawking at something that couldn't be worth more than its weight in scrap metal?

Sally Anne wasn't in her usual spot at the bar, but I spotted her coming out of her office, so I quickly made my way to her.

"Is everything alright, sweetie?" she asked. "I was just checking on inventory. I wanted to make sure we had enough booze and food to cover this unexpected rush."

"I don't think you're gonna have to worry about that tonight," I said sheepishly.

"Why's that?" she asked.

"Take a look at the tables, and the bar. You notice anything missing?"

Sally Anne scanned the room. "Sweet and sour Jesus. Why isn't anybody drinking?"

Sally Anne's hand flew to her mouth. "Sorry, hon, I know you don't like blasphemy."

"Don't worry about it, besides I don't think Jesus is your problem tonight," I said.

"Well, someone is keeping these healthy men from knockin' 'em back."

"The Magic Lady," I replied.

"Who the fuck is that, and do I have to cut the bitch?"

"She's part two of tonight's bad news report. These fine *gentlemen*, I can only assume because I have yet to see a female among them, are pinball nerds," I explained.

"Pinball nerds?" Sally Anne asked.

"*Sober* pinball nerds," I replied.

"And why are they here in my bar?"

"The Magic Lady."

As if on cue, the group in the corner erupted into cheers, and then broke apart as each of its members began congratulating the man in the center of it all. The crowd were all smiles, handshakes, and pats on the back for the man who I could now see was the one who must have been playing the Magic Lady pinball machine.

"I believe that's Troy, the group's leader," I said to Sally Anne, who immediately turned toward the source of the action.

"Let's go have a chat with Troy," Sally Anne said, and I fell in step right behind her as we made our way to Troy and his merry band of water drinkers.

As we approached the group, Sally Anne extended a hand to the man at the center. "Hello, my name is Sally Anne, and this is my bar. Are you Troy?"

"That's right, Troy Holden," he said, smiling. "It's so nice to meet a fellow pinball enthusiast. I can't believe you have a Magic Lady machine out here for everyone to play."

"Well, I'm not," Sally Anne said.

"Not what?" Troy asked.

"A pinball *enthusiast*. I am, however, an alcoholic beverage sales *enthusiast*, thus the reason I own a bar. True, it does have a pinball machine in it, but that was given to me around the time I bought the place, and I was under the impression that it didn't work properly," she said.

"Of course, it doesn't work properly!" Troy shouted gleefully to laughs all around. "None of them did. That's part of the charm of the Magic Lady and her legacy… I'm sorry, did you say that someone *gave* this machine to you?"

"Yes, but I feel like we're still talking about the pinball game and I need to talk to you about the very large group of sober men currently draining my club soda taps dry."

"I'll give you a thousand dollars for the Magic Lady machine right now," Troy said, in an 'I'm using my big boy voice' sort of way, and an eerie hush fell over the bar.

TWO

BURNING SAINTS

Ropes

"**D**ID CLUTCH PUT you up to this?" Minus asked with a laugh, before breathing out a huge sigh. "Shit, man, that was pretty good. You kept a straight face the whole time and everything. I'm impressed."

"I've self-published five books over the past four years and my readership is really starting to pick up steam," I replied.

"Let me guess," he said, still smiling. "You write stories about… sexy-ass vampires. No, wait… cowboys. That's how come all the questions about my boots."

"I write about a motorcycle club," I said.

Minus stopped laughing. "Are you fucking serious?" he asked.

"I can show you the book I'm working on right now. That's what I was doing out there in the hallway. I write every chance I get. It's like an addiction."

"Jesus, you are fucking serious. You're actually writing romance books about our club?"

"*A* club, not *our* club," I corrected. "Usually... but I'm working on something a little different right now."

"You write books as Ropes Kimble and people are able to buy them?"

"Yes, people can and do buy them, but I don't write as Ropes, and I sure as hell don't use my family name," I replied. "I use a pen name."

"A pen name? What is it?" Minus asked.

"You're just gonna give me shit about it."

"Look, brother. You're the one who brought this whole thing up. I don't know why, but you did," he said.

"You're right," I said, rising to my feet. "I don't know why I brought it up either. This was a mistake. Forget I ever said anything.

"C'mon man, don't get all bent out of shape."

"I said forget it. I'll bring you another idea."

"Hold on," Minus said softly. "I'm sorry, man. You just kind of caught me off guard. I've been prepared for guys to come at me ideas, ranging from pawn shops to pet shops, but I can't say I was ready for this."

I sat back down. "Look, I get it. It's why I've been nervous to talk to you about this."

"You of all people, I just didn't have you pegged as a pervert," he laughed.

"How does writing romance novels make me a pervert?"

"Aren't those books just stories about a bunch of horny motherfuckers... fucking?" he asked.

"Well, when you put it so eloquently..."

"You know what I mean," he said.

"No, I don't. And you don't know what the fuck you're talking about," I said.

He crossed his arms and leaned back in his chair. "What do you mean?"

"Have you ever even read a romance novel?" I asked.

"Fuck no," Minus snapped.

"Then how the hell do you know what's in them or that you wouldn't enjoy reading one yourself?" I challenged.

"Ropes, you're one of the only literate members of the Saints, let alone someone I can discuss the classics with. You've read everything from Nietzsche to Nabokov. Why in the world would you read that shit... let alone *write* it?"

"For such a well-read man yourself, I'm surprised at the level of your snobbery."

"I'm not a fuckin' snob," Minus said.

"Then read one of my books and tell me what you think."

"How the fuck am I supposed to tell if you have the ability to earn serious money as a romance writer? You're supposed to be selling me on the idea."

"I know I can make money, I already am, but that's not the point..."

"You really see money from writing these books?" Minus's tone shifted from disbelief to intrigue.

I reached into my satchel, produced a paperback, and handed it to Minus.

"This book is the first in my MC series. Read it and tell me what you think of the story. That's all I want you to do."

Minus looked at the book's cover and raised an eyebrow. "Clay Morningwood?"

* * *

Devlin

I didn't know what the hell had just happened, but it clearly got the attention of every weirdo in the bar.

"You wanna give me a thousand dollars for an old broken pinball machine?" Sally Anne asked.

"I'll write you a check right now," Troy said, reaching for his back pocket.

"Hold up there, GameBoy," I said, raising my hand.

"First of all, whenever negotiating a deal in a bar, be a man and bring cash. Second, if you're willing to pay one thousand for the machine, then I'm sure you'd be willing to pay two thousand."

"Two thousand?" Troy protested.

"I heard some of your little gang talking about how rare that particular machine is, so I figure it's gotta be worth more than you're letting on. We should probably have it appraised, Sally Anne."

"You're crazy. One thousand is a solid offer," Troy replied, his upper lip drenched in sweat. "I...I...I'll go to twelve-hundred, *caaaashhh*, just to prove that I'm serious.

I looked at Sally Anne who simply shrugged back. My phone was in my locker, per Sally Anne's strict on-shift rules, so I couldn't do a search on the game's value, but twelve hundred bucks of pure profit for a busted pinball machine seemed like a pretty good deal to me. Especially if it got these assholes out of our bar.

"Fifteen hundred," I said, quickly adding, "Plus, you and your boys haul it, and your non-drinking asses out of here."

Troy's eyes squinted before he smiled and extended his hand to seal the deal. I scanned the room for expressions that would show indications that we were getting fleeced but saw only stone faces. What did it matter anyway? In the end, what were we losing? A stupid pinball machine that no one played and only took up space? Fifteen hundred seemed liked more than enough to make up for the lack of a bar tab from these weirdos. I figured what the hell, and after a few moments of final deliberations, reached out to shake Troy's (more than likely sweaty) hand.

"I wouldn't do that!" a familiar voice blared through the otherwise totally silent bar. I turned to see Ropes, one of the Burning Saints, begin making his way toward us from the rear of the bar.

"Do what?" I asked, taken aback by the interruption.

"Shake that man's hand," Ropes replied.

Ropes was gorgeous. Not just hot for a biker, but GQ kind of hot. In fact, a good chunk of the Burning Saints club looked like they could pose for a charity calendar, but Ropes was next level good looking. He'd asked me to go out with him at least half a dozen times since I'd started working at Sally Anne's, and despite his looks and general politeness, I'd turned him down every single time. It's not that my pussy didn't want to accept his invitation, because believe me, it most certainly did, but I could not allow myself to become distracted from my goals right now, and I had a feeling Ropes would be a *big* distraction. At least that was the current line of bullshit I was trying to sell myself. I knew that I was terrified to let any man close to me after what happened with Tripp.

Ropes wore designer jeans, boots, and what looked like a tailored button up shirt, and jacket. It wasn't that far off from how he normally dressed, except for the lack of his leather kutte. I could see how his current lack of biker attire could cause Troy to mistake Ropes for a businessman, or male model rather than a guy who spent most of his time with his hands covered in either oil or blood.

"Do I know you?" Troy asked, his voice dripping with disdain.

"No, but I know who you are and how you do business, so I'm gonna suggest you haul ass out of here before you *do* find out who I am," Ropes said.

"Excuse me. Thanks, but I don't need any help," I said, a little irritated that Ropes had inserted himself into the middle of my conversation, let alone our deal.

"I never thought you needed help," Ropes said, flashing me a grin. "I merely wanted to make sure you didn't shake this slime ball's hand, and to let Troy know that we won't be accepting whatever chicken-shit, lowball offer he's made."

"*We?*" I asked.

"The Burning Saints own half of the bar, so yes, we," he said matter-of-factly. I looked over at Sally Anne and shrugged. She rolled her eyes and then made the universal "jack off" hand motion. I stifled a laugh.

Troy began to speak, but Ropes and I shushed him simultaneously before I continued.

"Like I said, I appreciate the assistance, but Troy just wants to buy that broken pinball machine."

"I know why he's here. I saw his post online about bringing his club here tonight. I was wondering how long it would take for word to get out about the machine being here," Ropes said. "I'd planned on getting here before they arrived, but I got held up in a meeting."

"Hold on," I snapped. "You're one of these guys?"

"I lurk on a few on-line forums," Ropes said.

"What the hell is going on here?" I knew that nerd culture was spreading, but a biker bar was the last place in the world I'd expected it to rear its pointed ears.

"I have an interest in the value of collectable arcade games," he replied.

"I don't know who you are," Troy said snidely.

"That's because I've never wanted to know you and I'd sure as hell never do business with you, so like I said..."

"Wait a minute," I interrupted. "You said, Troy had made a lowball offer, but you weren't here, so how could you know what his offer was?"

"I don't have to know what it was. If it came from him, it was a low-ball," he replied. "Troy Holden, aka PimpBall-Wizard, is a known scumbag within the community of serious buyers, who's known for ripping people off who don't know the value of what they own. His mindless cronies here do nothing about it, because even though he's an asshole, he's got connections and gets solid leads on inventory."

Troy once again opened his mouth to protest, but I bowled over him with my ranting, which was now directed entirely at Ropes.

"Did you think that maybe I accounted for him lowballing me, and had raised the price from his initial offer accordingly? *Twice*." I said.

"Oh, okay," Ropes said stepping aside, hands raised in surrender. "I hadn't realized, my apologies."

"Thank you," I said.

"As long as you settled somewhere near the twenty-grand mark then you're good, but you know what you're doing."

"Tw… Twenty…" I couldn't even complete the sentence. Troy's face sank, and the blood drained from his face. He knew the jig was up and that his deal was blown, and I knew that Ropes had been right all along.

"You're telling me that stupid pinball game…"

"Machine," the room corrected me in unison.

"Shut the fuck up, nerds!" I shouted. "You're telling me that stupid pinball *machine* is worth twenty thousand dollars?" I asked Ropes.

"At least," he replied.

"What's it doing here?" I asked.

"I didn't have anywhere else to put it," he replied.

The casual nature in which Ropes delivered this bit of information made me want to stab him in his beautiful face. "That's *your* pinball machine?"

"Well, it was until I donated it to the bar. I figured why put it in storage when people could play it. Granted, it's not the greatest game ever, but it's good for a few laughs after too many beers."

I stood stunned and silent for several moments, thinking of just the right words before settling on, "Listen up! I need everyone within the sound of my voice who's seen all of the Harry Potter movies to please get the fuck out of this bar immediately!"

The sound of grumbles and scooting chairs filled the room as the disappointed patrons made their way to the nearest exits. All except Troy that is, who stood motionless, his eyes fixed on me.

"I think you heard the lady," Ropes said taking a step toward him, but Troy refused to acknowledge him.

"I don't like liars," Troy said in a flat tone that gave me the creeps, before walking off to join the rest of his sad posse as they began to file out of the bar.

Once Sally Anne's had been cleared of all dungeon masters and black-market games dealers, I turned to Ropes, shoved a finger in his face, and snapped, "Sally Anne's office, now!"

THREE

BURNING SAINTS

Ropes

DEVLIN WAS PISSED. I didn't know her well enough to know *just* how pissed, but I knew women enough to read that her mood was currently set somewhere between Alien and Predator, and that I'd better do as I was told.

"Yes ma'am," I said and took a single step before Devlin dug one of her fire engine red fingernails into my chest.

"Don't call me ma'am, *ever*," she said.

I chuckled, "Sorry, I just…"

"I mean it," she said, digging in further.

It was clear that she wasn't fucking around, so I dropped my smile. "Got it," I said.

Devlin stepped to the side, which was a shame because I had a great view of her tits when she was standing in front of me. I barely felt the sting of her nail in my sternum when I had her glorious body to look at. I marched to the office and Devlin followed, closing the door behind us before immediately laying into me.

"Who the actual fuck do you think you are?" she snapped.

"I'm pretty sure I'm the guy who just saved you from getting ripped off," I replied. "So, you're welcome."

Devlin stood silently, arms crossed.

"I think the words you're looking for are, *thank you very much, Ropes*," I said brightly.

She huffed. "Fuck you very much, asshole."

"*Excuse me?*"

"No, I will not excuse you, or your behavior. I did not need your help out there and I do not appreciate you inserting yourself into my business."

"First of all, I think it's crystal clear that you *absolutely* needed my help. Secondly, and perhaps most importantly," I said taking a step closer. "You'd know, and very much appreciate it, if I were to actually insert myself into your business."

"Ropes, I've made it clear to you on several occasions that I'm not interested in being your backseat bitch," she said in a low, controlled tone. "The fact that you'd choose this moment to hit on me, weakly, I might add, is just one of the many reasons why I would never let you anywhere near my business."

I fully admit that my line was cheaper than usual and ill-timed, but Devlin was usually a good sport when I fucked around with her like this. She'd been on my radar since the day she'd started at Sally Anne's. I happened to be here on her first night and didn't think she'd make it to the end of the shift. She didn't know how to pull a beer tap or make change and looked like she'd rather be anywhere but here, but she could handle herself in a room full of bikers and that was most important. Plus, she was the only one who had ever figured out how to work the ancient relic that Sally Anne called a cash register. She'd picked it up at an estate sale because it looked cool, but until Devlin came along with her magic touch, it had been the most expensive paperweight the bar had ever purchased. She was clearly smart, capable, and she was without a doubt, the sexiest woman I'd ever seen. My draw to her was undeniable and I couldn't help myself from teasing her whenever she was around. I felt some sort of compulsion to annoy her as if we were kids on a schoolyard.

However, Devlin was no little girl, she was all woman, and right now she wasn't playing games, she was truly angry.

"Look, I'm sorry," I said, trying to reset the conversation, but it was too late. Devlin was set to chew my ass, and I was gonna have to stand here and take it. Normally I'd have split long ago, but I wanted to get to know her, so if this was what it took to have her undivided attention for a few minutes, I'd suffer through it.

"I understand that your club owns part of the bar, and that you guys basically have the run of the place, but from what I understand, all business decisions are to be made by Sally Anne herself. We were in the middle of a business negotiation, so you should have stayed out of it," Devlin said.

"*I should have stayed out of it*? You said it yourself, business calls are to be made by Sally Anne. Is your name Sally Anne?"

"No, but I was speaking for her... on her behalf," Devlin replied defiantly.

"On her behalf? She was standing two feet away from you. Couldn't she speak?"

"Of course, but these guys were sitting in my section and they were talking about the Magic Lady, and everything kind of escalated from there. Troy made an offer, and I just kind of went for it."

"On Sally Anne's behalf?" I asked.

"She gave me the nod!" Devlin exclaimed.

"The nod?"

"Yes."

"Was that the 'steal second base' nod, or the 'mafia hit' nod?"

"The, 'I trust you to handle this' nod, jackass."

"It looked like you were trying to run the deal and were getting your ass handed to you," I replied dryly.

"What the fuck do you know?" she shouted back at me. I was clearly not scoring any points with her, but I was now very curious as to why she was so invested in tonight's events and had a feeling I was going to have to push Devlin's buttons a little if I had a chance at getting a glimpse into her mind. What the hell did I have to lose?

"Clearly, I know a hell of a lot more about business negotiations than you do," I said with a smile.

Devlin didn't return the smile, but paused before asking, "Does that pinball machine really belong to you?"

"It did, before I donated it."

"Strange."

"Why is it strange for a person to own a pinball machine?"

"It's not," she replied. "It's odd for a twenty-something-year-old biker to own a twenty-thousand-dollar pinball machine. It's even weirder for that biker to park something so valuable in the corner of a bar."

"Like I said before, there's a lot that goes on around here that you don't know the first thing about."

"Why are you called Ropes?" Devlin asked, completely changing gears.

"Why do you want to know about that now?" I asked, perplexed at her new line of questioning.

"Never mind why I want to know. I just do," she replied.

"Jesus, you're a bossy one, aren't you?" I retorted to which Devlin scowled. "I'm called Ropes because that's the name my club gave me."

"I understand the concept of earning a club name. I'm asking how you got it."

"Why are you being so hostile to me?" I asked softly.

"I'm hostile because I'm pissed at you," she replied,

looking puzzled.

"No, you're not."

"What do you mean? Yes, I am. I just told you I am. I'm angry at you, that's why I'm yelling," she said, the volume level of her voice rising.

"Go out with me."

"What? Didn't you hear everything I just said? I'm pissed off at you and I'd never let you near me," she said, now looking utterly puzzled.

"No, you're not."

"Not what?"

"Pissed off at me," I replied smiling.

"Stop saying that!"

"Let me take you out tomorrow tonight and I'll tell you why I'm called Ropes, and why you aren't mad at me."

"I don't date clients," she said.

"Clients? This is a biker bar, not a law firm. You're a waitress for Christ's sake."

"First of all, that's the second time you've used the Lord's name in vain, and I'd ask that you not do it again in my presence, and secondly, I'm not a waitress, I'm a tattoo artist."

"A tattoo artist. Really?" I asked, ignoring the odd religious sentiment.

"Yes."

I suppose I wasn't too surprised, given the large amount of ink Devlin had on display, but I had no idea she was an artist herself.

"I'm predominantly waitressing, but I developed my dating practices while moonlighting at tattoo shops. As a rule, I don't date people I work with, co-workers or clients."

"Well, then, lucky for you, I fall somewhere in between," I said smiling but once again, got nothing in return. "Come on, Devlin, work with me here. I've been asking you out forever and you always shoot me down."

"That should have been a clear indication as to how I feel about you," she replied.

"See, that's the thing that's bugging me. You always say

no, so why is it that I always feel like you *want* to say yes?"

"Because syphilis is rotting your brain?" she replied without missing a beat.

I was trying desperately to keep my cool, which had suddenly become exceedingly difficult. This was the funniest shit anyone had ever said to my face and I could not let myself laugh. I turned away to keep her from seeing my struggle.

Suddenly, from behind me I heard, "Okay."

I whipped around, shocked at Devlin's sudden change of heart.

"We can go out tomorrow night, but I'm picking the time and place, meeting you there, and I'm paying for myself," she said, without a hint of warmth.

"Sounds romantic," I replied cheerily. "I'll give you my number..."

"I'll get it from Sally Anne," she said, and swung the office door open wide. "Goodnight."

"Goodnight then. I'll talk to you tomorrow," I said as I exited, but still very confused by the entire interaction.

"Can't wait," she said unconvincingly, turning around to give me a cheesy double thumbs up sign.

I needed a drink even more than when I'd walked in but thought it best if I got the fuck out of Sally Anne's place before Devlin changed her mind.

* * *

Devlin

Mental illness ran in my family, but it wasn't until that very moment that I'd ever worried about the health of my own brain. But, insanity was the only possible reason as to why I'd agreed to go out with Ropes. What else could explain how I'd come into the office to give him a piece of my mind, and instead walked out with a date. No, not a date. It couldn't be a date. I must make that point very clear to him.

Sally Anne was on me like white on rice the moment I stepped out of the office. "You okay sugar?"

"I think so, I'm not really sure, actually. No, I don't think I am."

"Everything okay between you and Ropes? He didn't do anything that warrants an ass kicking did he?"

Sally Anne was very protective of 'her boys,' but if any one of them got out of line in her place, they were gonna hear about it. She was tough as hell and didn't take shit from anyone but was also nurturing and genuinely sweet. Likewise, from what I'd seen, the Burning Saints were about as good a group of bikers you'd ever want to come across. They were tough and scary guys, but some of them, like Ropes, were warm and made me feel safe when I was around them. That was one of the main reasons I took this job in the first place, to be in a safe environment. A biker bar may seem like an odd place to feel safe, but after what I'd been through, I truly felt like there was no safer place for me to lay low while I earned the cash I needed.

"No." I sighed. "Ropes is fine."

"Fine doesn't begin to describe what that boy is," Sally Anne rasped. "If I were ten years younger, I'd have taken him into the office myself."

"Sally Anne!"

"What? Do you play for the other team sweetie?"

"No, it's not that. I brought him into the office to yell at him, not to jump his bones."

"Yell at him? For what? The way he saved your bacon back there, I figured you were in there on your knees giving him a proper thank you," she said with a chuckle.

"You are a horrible person," I replied.

"Maybe so, but I grew up salmon fishing with my dad, so I know when a fish is on the hook, and you've got that boy by the gills, Red."

"He asked me out again," I said.

"Of course, he did. He's not an idiot. Look at you. The two of you would have supermodel babies."

"Babies? Slow down there. It's just a date, or *not* a date."

"*You said yes?*" Sally Anne squeaked in delight, clapping her hands together rapidly like a little girl.

"Yes, but only to get him off my back about it. I think. Honestly, I don't know why I said yes." I huffed.

"Because you want him to take your little red kitty to the pound."

"Stop it!"

"You want him to drive his boat all the way to the *Bon-er*ville Dam."

"I swear to you, I'll quit this job tonight."

"You want to dance the horizontal mambo with him."

"I'm suing for sexual harassment. This is a hostile work environment."

The rest of the night was uneventful. We closed the place up a little early and got out of there just after two in the morning. I walked Sally Anne to her car before climbing into mine, which was nestled in its usual spot, backed against the cyclone fence.

I turned the key to the first position in the ignition and the sounds of La Boheme flooded the interior of Ben, my beloved Volkswagen Thing. I'd had him since art school, where I'd also fallen in love with classical music.

Puccini's masterpiece was my all-time favorite opera, and I remained parked in the darkness for several minutes, eyes closed, as the music washed over me. A welcome stress reliever after a long and bizarre day. When the piece ended, I flipped on my headlights and jumped in my seat. Troy was standing directly in front of my car.

I've heard a lot of talk about the 'fight or flight' instinct within every human, but there's a third option that often goes unmentioned, freeze. I was frozen stiff. My hands felt as if they were glued to the steering wheel and I could barely breathe.

Troy stood motionless, hands at his side, as the car's headlights cast an eerie shadow across his expressionless face. His greasy hair was matted to a sweat-covered fore-head. He looked like he was in some sort of fugue state.

After what felt like an eternity of staring into the face of my would-be killer, I found the strength to loosen my white-knuckle grip and I honked the horn, giving him one short blast. Troy didn't move a muscle or even blink.

I tried again, this time laying on the horn, and after a few moments of the blaring noise his facial expression finally did change.

He smiled.

I looked to the left and right of me, but mine was the only car in the parking lot. Sally Anne must have driven off while I was decompressing. Not her fault, she probably thought I was right behind her, but I wasn't. I was alone and about to be serial murdered in the parking lot of a biker bar. Worst of all, I was going to die with the knowledge that my mother had been right all along.

Troy finally broke his silence. "I don't like lying bitches."

"I don't like creeps. Get the fuck away from my car," I managed to squeak out the words.

"Or what?" was all he said.

"I… I'm going to call 911," I said, grabbing my purse from the passenger seat.

Troy slammed his fist down on the hood of my VW Thing. "I don't like liars and you're a dirty liar. We had a deal, bitch!" he shouted as I scrambled to find my phone.

Shit! Once again, I'd left my phone in my locker.

I stopped rummaging through my bag and looked up. Troy was now panting, practically foaming at the mouth, his eyes locked on mine.

"What's the matter, doll? Lost your phone?" He walked over to the driver-side window and licked it.

He fucking licked my window.

"You're gonna be my magic lady now."

I screamed and laid into the car's horn once again, my eyes instinctively shutting tight. When I finally looked up, Troy was gone. I glanced over my shoulder, then side-to-side, but could not see him anywhere. I took my hand off the horn for just a moment to see if I could tell where he was but could only hear muffled voices and grunts.

From the driver's side window, I could see someone in a Burning Saints' club kutte straddling Troy, who was pinned to the ground, flat on his back. Whoever the Saint was, he was relentlessly raining down punches from on top and didn't stop until Troy was a motionless lump.

As he stood and turned toward me, I could now see the Saint was Ropes.

"Are you okay?" he asked, breathless from the beating he'd just delivered, his hands dripping with blood.

"I... I think so."

"You need to take off before the cops show up. Someone may have heard your horn and called them already. I'll take care of this and check on you in just a bit. Drive straight home and don't stop for anyone."

I was so rattled I didn't even respond. I simply put the car into drive and sped off toward the freeway.

Ropes

"HEY, FUCKWAD, IF you don't want to bleed to death in this parking lot, I'd suggest you stand up and get some medical attention, pronto."

Troy had just regained consciousness and began moaning in pain.

"Quit making that sound right now before my boot heel puts you back to sleep," I said.

I collected what I could find of Troy's teeth and put them into my kutte pocket before leaning down and stuffing a one hundred-dollar bill into his bloodied mouth, causing him to writhe in pain. "This is a little something to go toward your dental bill. Now, get the fuck up and call one of your loser minions to come take you to the E.R," I said, before wiping the blood from my bruised knuckles. Nothing felt broken, but my hands were gonna feel like shit in the morning.

I walked to my bike and got on before adding, "When I told you earlier to stay away from Sally Anne's place, you must have thought I was joking. I don't hear you laughing right now, so I'm going to assume you now know that I was being deadly serious. Next time, I'm just gonna be deadly. Stay away from both my bar and my woman. If you even have a single thought about Devlin, I'll know it, and I'll come for the rest of your pearly yellows."

I cranked my bike and made sure I sprayed as much gravel as possible on Troy as I sped off in the direction Devlin had driven. I didn't even take the time to put my helmet on. I carefully pulled my phone out of my pocked and dialed Sally Anne, who picked up right away.

"It's late. You okay, sweetie?" she asked.

"Everything's fine, but I need Devlin's address right away," I shouted over the roar of my bike's engine."

"Doesn't the booty call usually come after the first date?" she asked with a raspy chuckle.

"It's not that. I really need it, Sally Anne."

"Hold on, let me get it for you," she said, and returned a few moments later with the address. "Are you sure everything's okay?"

"Thanks Sally Anne, I'll talk to you later," I said, ignoring her question, and hanging up.

I got on I-5 North and headed toward Vancouver, a suburban town in southern Washington, which was just across the Columbia River from Portland. Sally Anne's intel led me to the Happy Pines apartments, and I showed up on Devlin's second level doorstep to find her porch light off. I tried to peek into her front window, but no signs of movement from inside. I gently tapped on the front door and whispered, "Devlin, it's me, Ropes."

No response.

I tried again, this time a little louder. "Can you hear me? It's Ropes. Are you okay?"

Nothing.

I raised my volume to almost speaking level. "Devlin are you—"

Her door swung open, "Would you shut up? You're going to wake my neighbors," she whisper-shouted, and pulled me by my kutte, catching me off guard and causing me to stumble through her doorway.

* * *

Devlin

I tugged Ropes inside, then closed and locked my door. I was three shots of Grey Goose in and feeling the effects of the alcohol, which is probably why I virtually climbed his body to cover his mouth with mine.

At least this is what I planned to tell myself in the morning.

"Dev—"

"Hush," I hissed. "I know you want this and so do I, so come on."

"I think maybe you only want this because of what just happened."

"How about you let me decide what I want and why I want it."

"It's just—"

"I want your dick in my mouth, but your talking's gonna ruin it. So, I'd appreciate it if you'd zip it, so I can suck it."

"How about I unzip it?" he countered, his hands going to his jeans.

"Get to it," I demanded and knelt in front of him.

Ropes didn't waste any time… and neither did I, but again, he stopped me. "I'm clean, baby. Got the paperwork in my wallet, but I still want to use a condom."

I raised an eyebrow. "When it's time for your dick to migrate from my mouth to my pussy, you can use a condom, but I'd like it bare for my purposes."

"Fuck me."

"In a minute," I promised, tugging his jeans and boxers

down his legs. His cock sprang free and I gave myself a few seconds to marvel at the size. Jesus, he was big.

"We can wait," Ropes said, obviously mistaking my pause for trepidation.

"I'm just admiring the view," I said, then wrapped my lips around the tip.

He let out a hiss as I took him deeper, as far down my throat as I could without gagging. I wrapped one hand around the base of his shaft, cupping his balls with the other, then began to work his length with both my hand and my mouth.

His hands slid into my hair and he fell back against my door. I grinned when he began to fuck my mouth, and I added pressure to his shaft with my hand with each pass.

"Now, baby," he hissed out and tried to pull back.

I grabbed his ass and pulled him forward, glad he picked up on my need to taste him completely. He gripped my scalp harder and thrust once more before coming in my mouth. Before I could enjoy the effect I'd had on his body, he lifted me under my arms and pulled me up, kissing me as he yanked off my clothing.

"Your turn," he said, and I slid my hands up his chest.

Over the course of the night, Ropes repeatedly brought me to the edge of ecstasy and then pushed me over. By the time I fell asleep sprawled on his body, I was more drunk than tipsy, but I knew I'd never forget a second of the perfection of this night.

* * *

The birds outside sang a sweet melody, pulling me from my slumber, and despite my lower back being on fire, I felt well-rested. I rolled over to get into a more comfortable position and was confused to find that I had slept on the floor, a pillow and throw from the couch serving as my only bedding. Plus, I was naked as a grape and I *never* slept in the nude. I rolled onto my back to find a man's face directly over mine.

"Good mor—"

My right hand snapped forward reflexively, connecting

squarely with his nose, and he stumbled backward. I heard a massive crash from behind me and spun onto my stomach to see what the hell was going on. I let out a squeak and slapped a hand over my mouth.

Ropes was flat on his ass, blood gushing from his nose, covered in a mixture of orange juice, oatmeal, and egg yolks. A serving tray and an assortment of broken dishes were beside him on the floor.

I covered myself the best I could with the throw and shouted, "What the hell are you doing in my apartment?"

"What are you talking about, you maniac? I've been here all night. You begged me to stay. We had sex!" he replied.

Oh, shit. I had sex with Ropes last night. Really good sex.

"I know that," I said, trying and failing to somehow act and sound casual.

"Then why the fuck did you break my nose?" he demanded, now pinching the bridge of his nose with a napkin. His perfectly tatted chest, awash with blood and breakfast.

"I'm so sorry, it was just a reflex," I said, rising to my feet. "Here, let me help you up."

"I'm okay, Cherry," Ropes said. "I could use a couple of towels though."

"Cherry?" I asked.

"What?"

"My name's Devlin. You called me Cherry just now."

"I did? Sorry. I guess you rung my bell pretty good," he said.

"Let me get you some towels and an icepack," I said, feeling the heat of embarrassment creep up the back of my neck. "I'm just gonna put some clothes on really quick," I added, before darting into my room. I threw on some sweat shorts, smelled three t-shirts from atop the pile of dirty laundry, and selected the cleanest smelling one. I then ran out to the kitchen to find Ropes already there, standing at the sink, his ink-covered back to me. My knees buckled.

An outpouring of memories flooded my mind from last night. I'd never experienced that kind of sexual synergy before. Our bodies felt as if they were designed for one another and Ropes was able to take me to places I rarely visited. Now, in the light of the morning, and without the fog of alcohol, I could see his body was even more glorious than I knew.

"There are towels in the top drawer by your left hand," I said, and Ropes shot me a thumbs up without turning around. "I'm sorry about your nose. You scared the shit out of me."

"I understand," Ropes said, opening the drawer I'd directed him to only to find it empty, another glaring reminder that I was painfully behind on doing the laundry.

"Shit on a brick," I muttered. "Hold on one second." I ran to the bathroom, grabbed the cleanest bath towel I could find, and returned to wet, shirtless, Ropes.

"Thanks," he said, taking the towel. His nose appeared to have stopped bleeding but was swollen and already starting to bruise.

"Is it broken?"

"It wouldn't be the first time, but no, I think it'll be alright," he said smiling wide.

He was absolutely gorgeous. I can understand why, after last night's events and drinking too much, I could have lowered my defenses enough to sleep with Ropes, but I was still shocked that I did.

"Sorry about all of this," Ropes said, motioning to the carnage on the floor. "I made you a little breakfast, but I guess we'll have to settle for the freezer-burned toaster waffles I found earlier."

"You should go," I blurted out.

"What? Why? Did I do something wrong?" Ropes was still smiling, but he was clearly confused. I couldn't blame the guy, but on the other hand, I needed to process what the fuck had gone on within the past twenty-four hours or I was going to have a full-blown panic attack.

"No, you were great," I said, avoiding eye contact. I could feel my pulse starting to rise and my chest began to tighten. "I just, don't do… this kind of thing often. Like, as in, ever," I said.

"Oh, me neither," Ropes said in an assuring tone.

"Right," I snapped back sarcastically.

"Ouch," he said, dropping his smile. "That hurt more than the punch to my sniffer."

"Come on, don't act all innocent. You hook up all the time and you know it."

"You always make assumptions about people you don't know?" he asked.

"Are you saying you don't sleep around?"

Ropes took a step closer to me. "You didn't answer my question."

I swallowed. "What?"

"Are you in the habit of judging books by their covers?"

"No, but you've been on me since the minute Ben and I rolled into town, so I figured you must hit on everything with legs and boobs that walks into Sally Anne's."

"Have you ever seen me talking to any other women inside the bar? Or anywhere else, for that matter?" He took another step closer.

"No, but I—"

"Who's Ben?" he asked.

"W… what?"

"You said you and Ben rolled into town. Is he your boyfriend or something?"

"No, Ben is my car. A 1978 Pumpkin Orange Volkswagen Thing," I said. "I call him Ben after—"

"Ben Grimm of the Fantastic Four," Ropes finished my sentence, before taking my hand. My vision began to tunnel, and I felt like I was going to pass out. "Devlin, I've been asking you to go out with me since day one because I want to get to know *you*. I haven't even noticed other women since that day, let alone hooked up with anybody. I told you last night that I'm not with anybody, and I mean what I say."

I felt a wave of overstimulation hit me.

"You have to go now," I said, pulling my hand from his.

"Are we still on for tonight? I really do want to get to know you."

"I don't know. I'll call you later," I said still avoiding eye contact. Something about this guy made me feel very vulnerable and extremely uncomfortable.

"Can I help you clean up this mess?"

"Just go, please. I'm all right."

"Devlin, you don't seem all right."

Hearing Ropes say my name made me want to throw him on the kitchen floor and fuck him until I was raw, but mostly I just wanted to hide under a blanket in the fetal position and binge watch Bones with him.

Don't make eye contact.

"Devlin, please look at me," Ropes said softly.

I made eye contact.

Shit.

"Look, I don't know what that was all about last night," Ropes said, before quickly interjecting, "Don't get me wrong, it was amazing, but I feel like everything that happened at the bar and in the parking lot, last night may have… confused things between you and me just a little."

"Ya think?"

"Okay then." He smiled wide. "How about a Mulligan?"

"A Mulligan?"

"It's a golf term. It means a do-over."

"Golf? See, there you go again. What the hell kind of biker are you?"

"Let me take you out tonight like we'd planned and you can find out."

"We planned to go out together. I never said I'd let you take me out."

"What's the difference?"

"You 'taking me out' implies that you'll be doing things like picking me up, opening doors, and paying for everything."

"Does it?" he asked.

"Yes, it does, and none of that is going to happen."

"But we are still going out?" He flashed a boyish grin that I couldn't possibly refuse.

"Fine. I'll meet you at Pioneer Square Mall at seven."

"The mall?"

"Yes, there's a place there where I like to eat, so if you

want to go out with me, that's where I'll be."

"It's a date, then," Ropes said.

"No, it's not. It's just two people going out, paying via separate checks."

"One thousand pieces, no corners, no edges, give up now," Ropes said quietly.

"What?"

"Nothing," he said. "Just a memory from my childhood. I'll see you at seven."

"At the food court," I added.

"I'll be sure to reserve us a romantic spot with a view of the play area."

I managed to finally get Ropes out of my apartment, took one look at his failed attempt at sweetness that lay on my apartment floor, and burst into tears.

FIVE

BURNING SAINTS

Ropes

I T WAS BEFORE noon on a Sunday, so I figured most of
the Saints at the Sanctuary would be crashed out after a
hard night of partying. However, I was hoping Kitty, a
new house guest of ours was up. Kitty used to run with the
Dogs of Fire, a local club that we'd recently begun building
bridges with after years of tension. His staying with us was
likely going to cause our club some trouble as Kitty and the
Dogs of Fire did not part on the best terms. In fact, Kitty had
been told very clearly to leave Portland for good when he
was kicked out of the Dogs, but he'd helped us out of a serious jam a while ago, and the Burning Saints never left a debt
unpaid even if it meant we might catch a little hell for it. His
plan was to make good with his old club, but he'd settled in

with us quite nicely.

I pulled up to the Sanctuary gate and was buzzed in by the guard.

"Ropes! Where were you last night?" Doozer shouted as I entered the great hall of the Sanctuary. There were around a half-dozen Saints in the Sanctuary that I could see, but not the one I was looking for.

"Holy shit. Did you hit a fucking seagull on your bike this morning?" he asked, spotting Devlin's discount nose-job. He then glanced down at my bruised knuckles. "Oh, shit. You'd better not let Minus see those battle scars."

"I've been working out with the kids at Clutch's new place," I lied, using the boxing gym as an excuse.

"I never figured you for a guy who needed lessons on how to use his hands," he replied.

"We've all gotta stay in shape somehow, right? Is Kitty around?" I asked.

"I haven't seen him yet this morning. Maybe he's passed out somewhere," Doozer replied.

"Passed out? Did a tanker truck full of Jack Daniels show up last night?"

Doozer laughed. Kitty was massive, by far the largest in-dividual I'd ever met. It wasn't just his size that made him so dangerous, though. He was also a certified genius when it came to technology and I needed him to utilize those skills for me. I had what some might call trust issues. I'd also often been called a control freak, but I preferred the term "positive outcome enthusiast." I wanted to go into this date with Devlin with as much information as I could gather.

I made my way to Kitty's room and gently tapped on his door to no response. After a few seconds, I quietly cracked the door open and peeked inside. I had no desire to wake a sleeping giant, for fear of having a beanstalk shoved up my ass. As it turned out, I need not worry, as Kitty was wide awake, and balls deep in a busty blonde. He had his back to me and was taking her from behind. I couldn't even imagine how this chick was going to be able to walk later, but cur-rently she seemed to be enjoying herself just fine. This was worse than walking in on a sleeping Kitty, and I quickly shut the door, accidentally slamming it as I did.

"Who the fuck is there?" I heard Kitty bellow from behind the door.

"Um, it's Ropes. Sorry, man, I can come back later."

"Come on in brother!" he called back cheerily.

"It's okay, it sounds like you've got company."

"Get the fuck in here," he replied, and I did as I was told.

"Sorry to interrupt, but—"

"No problem, Mandy here doesn't mind, do you baby?"

"Um, my name is *Marny*," she corrected, still on all fours.

"See, she don't fuckin' care. What's up? Just make it quick. I don't wanna lose my boner."

"I just need some information about someone, a waitress who works at Sally Anne's. Anything you can find, really, and the sooner the better," I said, trying my best to avert my eyes from the happy couple.

"That all?" He chuckled. "Write the name down there on that pad and I'll have it for you in five...make, it ten minutes." He pointed to a notepad on top of his dresser by the door.

"Thanks, Kitty," I said, jotting down Devlin's name, then closing the door behind me.

I walked out to the great room, grabbed a beer from the cooler, and the first open chair I saw. It was only once I'd sat down and taken a few sips that I began thinking about what might have happened had I not gone back to the bar to talk to Devlin last night. I knew Sally Anne's usually closed at two o' clock on weeknights, but she was already in her car when I pulled up. It took me a few seconds to register what I was seeing, but as soon as I recognized Troy, I flew off my bike and was on top of him before I could even think. Although, the club was on a strict no violence diet, I knew even Minus would understand why I had to do what I did. At least I hoped he would, or I was in deep shit.

After a while I heard Kitty's booming voice. "Here you go," he said, holding out a single sheet of paper. I scowled as

I read its limited contents.

"Not much here," I said.

"Looks like there's not much to find," Kitty replied. "She was born in Idaho, moved here four years ago, and applied for a driver's license and tattoo permit the moment she got into town. No criminal record, no street affiliations and outside of student loan debt, seems clear."

I held up the paper. "Thanks, Kitty. I appreciate this."

"No problem, man. I don't know why you're looking into this chick, but she's clean as a whistle."

Surprisingly so.

I wasn't quite sure why Devlin's record coming back so clean made me feel uneasy. I suppose I was expecting Kitty to find an assortment of edges and barbs in her past and was simply caught off guard when he didn't.

"Thanks again, I owe you one," I said heading to the kitchen to grab another beer and an icepack before heading to my room.

As I got dressed, I remembered Troy's teeth in my kutte pocket and made a mental note to stop off at my mailbox later. A few years ago, I'd earned the nickname "Tooth Fairy" after I started mailing the teeth I'd knocked out back to their owners. It was my not-so-subtle way of reminding folks on the streets to stay in line. I wasn't a violent person by nature, but I certainly had a deep well of rage inside of me. A well that I could draw from when needed. My job as a soldier was to crack the skulls of the people who tried to strong-arm those under the club's protection. It was as simple as that, but I'd always rather deliver a message than a second beating whenever possible. Bloody molars via post seemed to do the trick.

* * *

Devlin

Sketching had always helped bring me back to the surface when I'd been dragged under by the waves of a panic attack. Art as therapy was what got me into drawing as a kid. I'd always suffered from episodes of severe anxiety from as far back as I can remember, but recent events had caused them to develop into crippling panic attacks.

Often, what I sketched during these times inspired some of my favorite tattoo designs, some of which have even made it onto clients. Today, my creative subconscious and colored pencils led me to sketching mostly eyes. Reaching for various hues of green, eventually finding the right balance between emerald and jade, before realizing I was sketching eyes that belonged to a face I knew. These were Ropes's eyes.

"Gimmie a break," I cried out and flopped over on the sofa.

I had no idea how or why this guy had gotten under my skin, but there he was, nonetheless, a beautiful splinter. Well, maybe I had some idea. He was impossibly good looking, sexy, and he saved me from possibly being on the next episode of Dateline. But still, to sleep with him like that. What was I thinking? He probably thinks I'm a slut now and has lost all respect for me anyway, so what does it matter? He'll be calling at any minute to cancel tonight, just wait and see.

Any minute now.

SIX

BURNING SAINTS

Ropes

I PULLED INTO the mall's parking structure and found a safe place to park my bike. I turned off the ignition and let out a heavy sigh. Shopping centers were on a short list of places I dreaded going to. I saw them as temples built to worship brand name gods. Repositories designed to collect the unholy tithes of the poor, unwitting victims of the church of capitalism. It was places like this that helped build my grandfather's empire and I normally avoided them at all costs, but this was the place Devlin wanted to go, so here I was.

In truth, there was one bright spot in this place and I planned on stopping in before I left. I took the elevator to the second floor and made my way into the belly of the beast.

The smell of the mall's interior was like that of every other I'd been in... a mixture of shoe leather, soft pretzels, and scented candles. It was only as I approached the food court that the smell began to change, in that it got even worse. On top of the original smell, we could now add the stench of over a dozen sub-par eateries and their poor attempts at global cuisine.

I looked around and, like a flower in the desert, I spotted Devlin sitting at a two-top, directly in the center of the food court, surrounded by suburbanite families busy stuffing their faces while gawking mindlessly at their smartphones.

"Have you been waiting long?" I asked as I approached.

"Just a few minutes," she replied, smiling only slightly, her hands folded neatly on top of the table, a funky green vintage handbag on her lap.

"Oh good," I said. I was on time, but Devlin having already arrived made me feel like I was late, and therefore like a tool. "Let me start off by saying how wrong I was about this place. Had I known about the romantic ambiance, I'd have taken all my dates here."

"This isn't a date," Devlin shot back, dropping what little smile she'd had.

"Okay, then, just two people having dinner."

"Right."

"So, what's on the menu tonight?" I asked cheerily, trying to get us back on track. "Taco Charlie's or Cup O' Pizza?"

"Derby's," Devlin replied.

"Derby's?" I asked, apparently unable to hide the disdain in my voice.

"Is that a problem?"

"What? No, Derby's is great," I replied as straight faced as possible.

Derby's was not great. Derby's had to be the worst burger chain in the entire country. So bad, in fact, that there's only a half-dozen of them left, and yet, of all the places in the world, this is where Devlin wanted to eat.

"Good. You watch the table while I go order, then we

can swap, and I'll wait for you," she said matter-of-factly.

"I'll be happy to wait in line with you, besides, this is my treat." I said.

"I told you, this isn't a date and I'll pay for myself. I agreed to go out with you, but not *out* with you."

"You do know that we fucked last night, right?" I asked, apparently a little too loud for her liking.

"Shhhhhhh, there are kids all around us."

"I know I asked for a Mulligan, but do we have to act like complete strangers? I get that you're a strong independent woman and all, and I'm not trying to step on the vibe you've got going, but why can't you just let me take you out?"

"I *can*, but I'm choosing not to. This is not a date."

"You've made that very clear."

"Apparently not, because you keep trying to turn it into one."

"I'm confused," I said.

"And I'm hungry, so save our table and I'll be back with my food."

"Oh, do they serve food at Derby's now?"

Devlin didn't reply. She turned sharply on her heels and walked toward the order line, leaving me with a view of the most perfect ass I'd ever seen. Last night was such a blur of activity that I'd barely had time to savor Devlin's body the way I'd wanted to. Next time I'd take my time, if there was even going to be a next time. Right now, I couldn't tell what Devlin's angle was. She'd agreed to going out, which had to mean something, but now she was sending me very clear signals to slow down, if not back the fuck off entirely. She was perfectly fine with letting me put my dick into her but paying for her cheeseburger was somehow off limits. I hadn't figured out her thought process yet, but I was gonna crack her code if it killed me.

The same childhood memory I'd had last night came rushing back along with a foggy black and white image.

One thousand pieces. No corners, no edges, give up now.

After a few minutes, Devlin returned with her meal. Two

fully loaded cheeseburgers and a mountain of French fries drenched in bright orange goo. As if that weren't enough, she also had onion rings, and a strawberry milkshake, complete with whipped cream and a cherry on top.

"Okay, your turn," she said, carefully setting the tray on the table.

"Jesus. Are you sure there's anything left in the kitchen?" I replied.

"I've asked you not to use the Lord's name in vain."

"I'm sorry," I replied. "I keep forgetting. I guess you just don't strike me as the religious type."

"I'm not." she said. "And I swear like a sailor otherwise, but blasphemy is just something I feel strongly about. Out of respect for some of the people who helped me out of a bad situation. The only people who ever helped me in my entire life, actually." She smiled softly.

"Maybe you can tell me about it some time," I said.

"Go get your food so I can eat," she said, clearly dodging my attempt to get on the inside.

"I'm good, you go ahead and eat."

"You're not going to get anything?"

"I'm kind of picky about what I eat," I replied.

"How can you possibly look at this tray and not want to tear into it?"

"Maybe the fact that it's covered in asbestos. Not to mention, I try to avoid eating anything served on a tray."

"What's wrong with food on trays?"

"What's *right* about it? Dining room trays are for prisons, schools, and mental hospitals."

"And surfing," Devlin added.

"What?"

"Don't tell me you've never been Derby's Surfing."

I shook my head.

"In high school, me and my friends would cut class and go to the Derby's about a mile away. We'd pool our money together, split an order of sloppy fries and then use the tray to go surfing."

I stared blankly at Devlin.

"Oh, come on! I can't believe you've never done this. You stand on the tray, crouched down low while holding onto the rear bumper of a friend's car. Then they drive around, while you surf the parking lot. The set's over when the asphalt chews up the surfer's tray or their knees."

I smiled, happy that Devlin had shared something about her life with me. Perhaps I'd be able to turn this evening into a date after all. "Sounds fun."

"You had to jump on any chance to have a good time for free when you grew up poor, right?" Devlin smiled.

"Uh, sure," I said and changed the subject. "So, what do you want to do after we eat?"

"You mean, after you watch me eat like some sort of deranged lunatic?" She laughed before turning serious. "Speaking of deranged lunatics, I want to thank you for saving me—"

"I didn't save you," I said.

"It sure as hell felt like it from where I was sitting. I don't know why I didn't act sooner, or just run him over. I was frozen. It took so long just to figure out what the hell Troy was doing there."

"I'm just glad I was there when I was."

"Me too." Devlin paused and screwed up her face. "Why were you there anyway?"

"Why the what now?" I sputtered.

"What were you doing in the parking lot of Sally Anne's so late? You'd left hours before that and the bar was closed, so what were you doing?"

"You know what? Suddenly I'm craving clam nuggets. I think I *will* go get in line," I said rising to my feet.

"Hold on there, bub, sit back down," she said, and I did as instructed.

I didn't know if I should tell her that the reason I went back to Sally Anne's was to talk to her. I didn't want to come off like some sort of stalker, especially after what she'd just been through with Troy. On the other hand, I didn't want to lie to her. There was something about Devlin that forced me to be completely honest. Maybe it was because she was so straightforward herself, but I felt it was very easy to cut straight through the bullshit with her, and so I came clean.

"I went back to Sally Anne's because I wanted to talk to you," I said.

"Why? I'd already agreed to go out with you."

"That's the thing. I was gonna call it off."

She paused midway through stuffing a wad of fries in her mouth. "You were gonna bail? After all your pestering and begging?"

"I never begged."

"You totally begged."

"I wasn't going to bail. I felt bad about the way I asked you out. It was shitty timing and I felt like you only said yes to get me off your back, so I was going to give you an out."

Devlin removed the cherry from her milkshake by the stem and took it into her mouth slowly. "I can't seem to figure you out."

"Me?" I asked, completely distracted by what I was seeing. Devlin's tongue around that cherry caused a rush of blood to my cock and flood of inspiration to my brain.

"I see you in the bar with your club all the time, and you never quite seem to fit in with them, do you?"

"What do you mean?"

"Most of the Burning Saints that I've seen look like bikers. They're gruff, mono-syllabic, hairy dudes."

"And?"

"And, you look like a men's fragrance ad model."

"Jesu—" I stopped myself. "You're quite direct, aren't you?"

"I can't stand lying," she said plainly.

"What does you blurting out whatever is on your mind have to do with honesty?"

"I guess I feel like if I'm not saying what I'm thinking, then I'm lying."

"That's the stupidest fucking thing I've ever heard in my entire life."

"Excuse me?" Devlin raised an eyebrow.

"Some thoughts should remain thoughts, and some earn the right to be said out loud. Occasionally, a thought is special enough to write down, but most of the time, that shit should stay locked up within the grey matter."

"Don't you feel like a phony when someone asks you a question and you aren't completely honest with them?"

"It would depend entirely on the question and who was asking it," I replied.

"Not for me."

"Really? The truth is that black and white for you?"

"Life *is* that black and white for me, and you never answered my question."

"I'm sorry, was there a question somewhere within your ethics lecture?" I asked, smiling.

Devlin dipped an onion ring in her milkshake before biting into it with a loud crunch. "So, why don't you fit in with your club?"

"Why don't you have better table manners?"

"Stop deflecting," she said between chews.

"I have no idea what you're talking about. The Burning Saints are my brothers and I'd die for any one of them."

"Sure, sure, I get all that. Brotherhood, bro-code, yada yada," she said with a dismissive wave.

"Hold on," I said, feeling the heat of anger creep up the back of my neck. The cat and mouse game we were playing had taken a turn I didn't much care for. "You can say what you want, or make any assumptions you want about me, but don't drag my club or my brothers into it."

"I'm sorry—"

"I'm not done. I don't know what you're driving at with these questions, or why you've got your guard up, but I didn't ask you out tonight because I needed a sparring partner. I asked you out because I find you fascinating, and I want to get to know you better."

"What do you mean my guard is up?"

Just then a vision of penguins flooded my mind.

"One thousand pieces, no corners, no edges, give up now," I said.

"You said that before. What is that?"

"Do you know what they call a group of penguins?" I asked.

"What the fuck are you talking about?" she burst out.

"Shhhh, there are children present," I chided. "They're called a raft."

"That's fascinating, but what does that have to do with me being guarded?"

"I learned that a group of penguins is called a raft off the back of a jigsaw puzzle in my grandparents' game room."

Devlin looked at me puzzled. "Game room?"

I ignored her question. "On the front of the box was a picture of the largest known raft of penguins in Antarctica. Also, on the front, printed in bold red letters were the words: 'One thousand pieces, no corners, no edges, give up now.' I suppose it was meant to intimidate, therefore entice puzzle enthusiasts. You remind me of that puzzle box. Everything about you screams stay away, but you bait your hooks nonetheless."

"Bait my hooks?"

"Sure. You're beautiful beyond words and you know it. The way you dress and carry yourself proves that, yet you pretend to be put off when I notice."

"I'm a pretender?" Devlin pointed a finger at me. "What about you?"

"What about me?"

"You use words like intimidate, therefore, and entice, and talk about your grandparents' game room. If I hadn't seen you wearing your kutte, I'd never guess in a million years that you were a biker, let alone in a hard-core club."

"So, I have a vocabulary, so what?"

"No, you have money."

I swallowed. "What the hell are you talking about?"

"You're rich. I can smell it on you. You're clearly well-educated. You're always dressed to the nines. You have a pinball machine worth twenty thousand dollars sitting in the corner of the bar collecting dust, and you tensed up when I mentioned knowing what it was like growing up poor."

"My family has money, so what?"

"I knew it," she said smugly.

"Don't turn this back around on me. These 'social judo' moves of yours, where you shift the weight of the conversation back onto the other person, is the kind of thing I'm talking about."

"What the hell do you know?"

"You're afraid to let people in."

Devlin wadded up her last napkin and tossed it on top of her half-obliterated meal. "You couldn't possibly have the slightest clue about who I am or what I'm about."

"You're a raft of penguins to me. I'm not afraid of your warning signs. Your hidden corners and edges don't intimidate me. When I look at you, I see the complete picture of who you are, even if I don't have all the details yet."

"Bullshit."

"Try me."

SEVEN

BURNING SAINTS

Devlin

T HIS ROPES GUY was officially starting to piss me off. Not just because he was a smug know-it-all, but because he was right about me putting my guard up. He'd already ruined every attempt I'd made to scare him off early and now he wanted to push my buttons? The thought of him pushing on anything at the moment made me want to hurl. I'd scarfed down that toxic barnyard of a meal right in front of him and he barely batted an eyelash.

"Ropes," I said with a sigh. "There's no way you could possibly know the first thing about me."

"Let's make a deal," he said, shifting tones. "If I can accurately state one true thing about you that no one knows, you'll agree to treat the rest of this evening like a date."

"Did you used to work at a carnival?"

"I'm not talking about something trivial like guessing your weight or age."

"You take a guess at either of those out loud and it'll be the last coherent thought you ever have, buddy."

"Do you agree? If I can prove to you that I know something about you—"

I rolled my eyes and threw my hands in the air. "Yes, then it's a stupid date, whatever."

Ropes smiled, and his eyes softened. He had the most amazing green eyes I'd ever seen. They were kind and trustworthy, and provided perhaps the biggest disconnect for me between Ropes the person and Ropes the biker.

"Wait!" I interrupted. "First, you have to tell me one thing about yourself. Why are you called Ropes?"

He chuckled. "Why is that important right now?"

"Is it a sex thing?" I blurted out.

"What? No," he laughed.

"I thought it might be a kinky sex thing and I guess I just wanted to know if I was safe with you."

Ropes took my hands, which were covered in cold sweat and Derby-Q sauce.

"Devlin. Nothing will ever happen to you when I'm around. Don't you trust me after last night?"

"No. I saw you beat a creep to a bloody pulp with your bare hands. Plus, for all I know, you paid him to be there in the first place." I pulled my hands from his. I was getting myself worked up and I wasn't sure why.

"Hold on, do you really think I'd do something like that?"

"I don't know, *Ropes.* I have no idea who you really are."

"Spencer. My real name is Spencer."

"Well that clears up the mystery," I shot back.

"I never tell anyone my real name. Ever."

My eyes met his and I could see the sincerity on his face. "Why?"

"Because it reminds me of my father and I hate my father, just like you hate yours.

My stomach dropped. "H… how could you know anything about my relationship with my father?"

"I told you I would tell you something true about yourself."

"But that's not true. My dad and I get along fine."

That was a lie. I had just extolled the virtues of telling the truth moments ago, then turned around and told a big old fat lie.

Ropes stood up, pushed his chair back and extending his hand. "Come on," he said with a smile.

"Where are we going?"

"To start our date. There's something I want to show you."

"But you didn't win!" I protested.

"Look, Devlin. We can call it a night right now and I'll never talk to you again, or you can cut the bullshit and start being honest with me. I know that we started off on a chaotic and bizarre note, but if you'll just trust me a little bit, I think you'll see that I'm a good guy."

"Why do they call you Ropes?"

"I'll tell you later, I promise. Come with me and I'll show you who I really am, or at least who I hope to be."

I took Ropes's hand and followed as he led me through the food court to the escalators.

"Where are we going?"

"Not far. We're not even going to leave the mall."

We walked hand-in-hand, passing store after store in complete silence. Ropes's ability to look right into my soul freaked the shit out of me, but I also felt comfortable around him. That's not to say that I felt safe, quite the contrary. I was a bundle of frayed nerve endings on roller skates. I couldn't believe I was letting him hold my hand and take jabs at me. I'd always said I wasn't attracted to 'yes men,' but this guy was able to push back without completely irritating me. He somehow knew how close to the edge he could push me, and I needed to know how and why he was able to do that. If I had a weak spot, a way for people to sneak in, I needed to know about it.

"Here we are," Ropes said, and we stopped in front of a large bookstore.

I crinkled my nose. "Alpine Books?"

"Sure, why not?"

"I thought you wanted this to be a date?"

"What, you don't think books are romantic?"

"I suppose it depends on the book. I'm not gonna get all hot and bothered over Olson's Standard Book of British Birds or something."

"What if it was the expurgated version?" he replied.

My head snapped, and my eyes locked on his. "The one without the Gannet?"

"They've ALL got the Gannet!" we exclaimed together in equally bad British accents before erupting into laughter.

"I quote Monty Python all the time and people have no idea what I'm talking about," I said, carefully wiping the tears from my eyes. "Okay, be honest," I said, tilting my head up toward the overhead lighting. "Is my mascara running?"

"No, you look beautiful. Perfect actually," Ropes said before tilting my head toward his. His lips covered mine and I gasped before returning his kiss. My heart was beating harder than when Troy was stalking me. I wanted to push away. No, that's not true. The last thing in the world I wanted to do was push away, and that's what scared me. Why was I letting this guy get close?

We finally broke our kiss and Ropes said, "I've been wanting to do that all night."

"This still isn't a date," I replied with a playful grin.

"C'mon," he said, and led us into the bookstore.

Alpine was one of the area's last true bookstores. This location wasn't as impressive as the original downtown store, but that one had been sold two years ago to make more condos. This truncated version of Alpine still managed to retain a very "Portland" feel, despite its surroundings. The eclectic nature of the city was well-represented, both by the store's décor, and its content. The shelves were stuffed with new and used books of every genre imaginable. Ropes led me by the hand through twists and turns until we reached a narrow spiral staircase that had been hand painted in bright day-glow colors.

"Where are you taking me?"

"You'll see," Ropes replied, leading me upstairs to a large loft area. The space was set up with over-stuffed furniture and bean-bag chairs. Vintage floor lamps lit the space and jazz music was playing lightly in the background. Several patrons sat, sipping coffee while reading.

"This is nice," I said. "Kind of quiet for my taste, but nice."

"This store is one of the two reasons I'd ever come to this or any other mall."

"What's the other reason?"

He looked back and smiled wide. "You."

I was going to need to buy some dry panties while I was at the mall.

"What I want to show you is over here," Ropes said, motioning to a group of large shelves located in the back corner of the room.

"You're not gonna show me a bunch of books about serial killers, are you? Please tell me you're not into all that creepy shit."

Ropes just smiled and led me to the section, which I could now see was marked "Romance and Erotica" and placed me directly in front of an endcap display for the 'Blazing Trails Series' by D.W. Foxblood.

"Here," he said, extending an arm toward the display.

"Here, what?"

"Look, it's clear to me that you're not gonna let me get any closer to the real you until you know what I'm all about, which is fair enough, so in order to speed things up a little, I wanted to show you who I want to be."

"You want to be a woman?" I said, pointing to the author's picture.

Ropes laughed and fired back playfully. "No, you lunatic, I don't want to be D.W. Foxblood, I want to be *like* D.W.

Foxblood. I want to write romance novels for a living."

"You're joking right?"

Ropes's smile dropped. "Why is that everyone's response?"

"You've told *other* people about this?"

A hard-core biker with aspirations of becoming a novelist was beyond my comprehension, let alone one who wanted to write some kissy-kissy Fabio shit.

"Actually, you're the second person I've said a word to about any of this. The only other person who knows is Minus."

Ropes's apparent vulnerability made me very uncomfortable. "Why are you telling me something so personal?"

"I told you, Devlin, I want to get to know the real you and likewise, I want you to get to know, and eventually trust me."

"Why is that so important to you? Why the rush to get inside my head? Why are you being so…pushy?"

Ropes took a step backward. "I don't mean to push."

"That's not what I meant. Not exactly anyway." I took a deep breath and collected my thoughts before starting over. "I like you, Ropes. I think that's pretty obvious by now, but I don't think we're on the same page."

"How so?"

"I told you before that I'm not focusing on my dating life right now and there are several reasons for that, but I will not bore you with those details. However, when I do date, I always take things slow. Very slow. *Painfully* slow. I certainly do not sleep with guys after the first date, let alone *before*," I said lowering my voice.

"Look, I hope you don't think that I—"

"I don't care what you do, and you don't owe me an apology. I would just like to make it clear that our sleeping together last night is not some sort of green light onto relationship avenue. I understand how that can be confusing, but it's what it is."

Ropes grinned. "Thanks for clearing all that up. Do you feel better now?"

"All I'm saying is that from my perspective, we are moving at warp speed, so why do I get the notion that you feel like we're crawling?"

Ropes paused for several seconds before saying "That's a really good question."

"Thank you," I replied, pausing in vain for him to add more. "Do you have an answer?"

"To what?"

"Ropes, to your knowledge has anyone been murdered inside Alpine Books before?"

"Not that I know of, but this is the romance section. Murder mysteries are downstairs."

I playfully smacked Ropes's chiseled chest. "Come on, knock it off."

"I told you already, Devlin, you're a raft of penguins to me. I see the whole picture of you already, but I need you to let me in."

"Why me? I'm sure you could sleep with any girl in Portland. Why are you so bothered with getting to know me?"

"First of all, you're no bother, and secondly, I'm not going after other women in Portland. I want to spend time with you and only you. Any way you want to do that, I'm down. If you want to talk, we can talk. If you need to fuck, I'll fuck you until you beg me to stop."

Ropes lifted my chin and kissed me again. This time I didn't resist at all, but instead allowed myself to lean into him as he explored my mouth with his tongue. He was an amazing kisser and I imagined him doing even more with that mouth.

The sound of a woman clearing her throat broke our kiss. "Excuse me, may I help you?"

We looked down to see a squatty young woman with bright pink horn-rimmed glasses looking up at us.

"Um, no I don't think so," Ropes replied. "I'm pretty sure I'm getting the hang of kissing this woman all by myself and don't require any assistance."

I gave Ropes another quick palm to the chest as I felt my cheeks begin to flush.

"I meant can I help you find a book?" the woman replied without a trace of merriment.

"Actually, yes. Do you have any advanced copies of Combustion by D.W. Foxblood?"

"That book doesn't come out until Tuesday," she replied.

"I understand," he said leaning down to read the woman's name tag, "Marlene, but I was hoping since that's in just a few days, that you might already have some copies in the back."

"Petal."

"Excuse me?"

"My name is Petal. You called me Marlene," the woman said.

"I'm sorry, it's just that your name tag says Marlene, so I thought—"

"This is Marlene's name tag, but I'm Petal, so…"

"Okay," Ropes said, sounding understandably confused. "I'm sorry I got your name wrong, but how could I have possibly known that you're not Marlene?"

"Because, she's not here tonight," she replied in her best "duh" tone.

Ropes blinked. "Do you have the book?"

"Yes," Not-Marlene replied, "But it doesn't—"

"Come out until Tuesday, yes I understand. Petal huh?" Ropes said, pulling a wad of cash from his pocket. "Your parents' hippies?" Ropes asked

"No, why?"

"I just thought maybe, because of the name…"

"I chose my own name," she replied dryly.

"Why ya sportin' Marlene's tag?" I interjected.

"Because I don't want anyone defining me, or telling me who I am."

"By calling you by the name you chose, for yourself?" I asked.

"*Exaaaclty.*"

"I for one am glad we've had this chat," Ropes said, peeling off two one-hundred-dollar bills and handing them to 'She who shall not be named.' "I'd like two copies of Combustion please and I don't need change back."

Two minutes later, Ropes had his books in a bag and we were heading out the door.

"What a whackadoo," I said as we laughed our way through the exit, towards the parking structure.

"Keep Portland Weird, right?"

"I prefer the bumper sticker that says, 'Keep Vancouver Normal.'"

"Get out of here," Ropes said.

"No, really. I like living in the 'Couve," I said.

"Seriously? You prefer living in Vancouver to Portland?"

"Sure, why not?"

"I guess I just figured with your vibe, you'd be a full-blown Portland chick, that's all."

I stopped our stroll. "That's the second time you've mentioned my appearance tonight."

"You didn't like it earlier when I said you were beautiful and perfect?"

"No, not that. That was fine. Earlier, in the food court. You said something about my look being a defense mechanism."

"I never used those words," Ropes corrected me.

"Okay, maybe not those words exactly, but something to that effect."

"Your armor is beautiful, but it's armor nonetheless."

"What's that supposed to mean?"

"*That* right there is what I want to get through," Ropes said with an intensity I'd not yet seen.

"What are you talking about?"

"You know exactly what I'm talking about. You are naturally beautiful in every way. Your face, your body, the way you move... all perfect." Heat crept up the back of my neck and I began to worry that my upper lip was sweating. "Yet, you're always dressed to kill, all your ink on display, and even though you're obviously a natural redhead, there's always an extra pop of color in your hair. You want attention and you get it, but your look also screams, 'Fuck off! You can't have me.' I think you know exactly what you're doing, but perhaps you don't know why just yet."

"Now who's judging a book by the cover?" I asked.

"That's not what I'm doing at all."

"Oh, really? I'm certainly feeling judged, and you're the only one talking to me right now," I snapped.

"I'm not judging you or your appearance, and if I were, honestly it's all working for me," Ropes said. "Big time."

"You need to work on your complimenting skills."

"I'm not trying to compliment or judge you, Devlin. I'm trying to understand you."

"Why do you want to understand me, Ropes?"

"Because you're my muse."

I stared at Ropes for a long while, trying to craft the appropriate response. What I ended up with was, "The fuck?"

EIGHT

BURNING SAINTS

Ropes

"**D**ON'T FREAK OUT," I said, following Darien up to her apartment. I'd practically white knuckled my drive here, worried she'd park her Thing, then try to keep me from coming in.

"What the fuck does that mean, Ropes? I'm your *muse*."

"Let's take this conversation inside," I said, and waved my hand toward her door.

"Explain," she pressed once we were inside.

"About two months ago, I was working on a book and getting nowhere fast."

"You really write romance novels? This isn't some sort of line?"

"Why is that so hard to believe? People of all types have

been writing books for eons."

"Sure, but I've never known a dude who wanted to write that kind of stuff for a living, let alone aspired to be the next D.W. Foxblood."

"So, you *do* know who she is."

"Of course, I do. I don't live on Mars." Devlin smiled. "I can't say I've read any of her books, seen the movies, or would be able to pick her out of a police line-up, but I am familiar with her work.

"Did you know her husband is in a club?"

"Really?"

"Yup. She doesn't talk much about her personal life in interviews, but I know her old man rides, and her books clearly pull from first-hand experience within an MC. When I first read her work, my eyes were opened to what could be done within this genre, that these books were more than just pulp."

"So where exactly do I fit into this picture?" I asked.

"A few months ago, for the first time ever, I was blocked, and it was affecting my life at every level."

"Blocked? As in writer's block?"

"Big time."

"You couldn't write at all?"

"I could write. I wrote every single day, I just hated everything I was putting down. To put it simply, I was uninspired and lacking vision." I took Devlin's hand and was relieved when she didn't pull away. "Two months ago, you walked into Sally Anne's and I wasn't blocked anymore. The moment I saw you, a new story was born, and a new character walked into my life."

"Are you telling me that you've been writing a story about me?"

"Cherry."

"Her name is *Cherry*? Is she a *stripper*?"

"A schoolteacher."

"Of course, she is," Devlin said dryly before letting go of my hand. "Look, Ropes, I'm sure many women would be really flattered by all this, but you're sort of freaking me out here. I'm kind of a private person and…"

I covered her mouth with mine and smiled against her lips when she sighed and leaned in to me.

"Ropes, we need to talk about this." Devlin protested with her words, but began writhing and grinding against me.

"I think we're done talking for now," I challenged.

"Maybe… maybe you're right," she rasped, and I kissed her again.

I slid a hand up to her neck and grasped her jaw. My other one dropped to her pussy and I cupped her over her jeans. She moaned and leaned in to my hands, and I kissed her gently as she moved against my palm.

I smiled against her mouth, giving her one more kiss. "Are you okay?"

"I'm amazing," she panted out.

"Do you want more?"

"I want it all, Ropes."

"You'll tell me if you want to stop."

She met my eyes and nodded. "I promise. But I like it fast and hard. Can you do that?"

"Yeah, baby, I can do that," I said, and made quick work of removing her clothes and pushing her gently over her sofa.

"Don't move," I ordered and stripped before rubbing a finger through her wet folds, my dick pulsing against her ass.

Her hips arched into my hand. "Ropes," she rasped.

"Tell me you know what I want." I slid my middle finger through her wetness again.

She shivered and pushed back into my cock. "I want your cock in my pussy."

"We can finish there." I shoved a finger inside her. "But I also want to show you how badly you ruin me when your pussy covers my dick." I shoved a second finger inside her tight heat. "And then, I want you to scream my name when you come."

She growled and arched her back. "Hurry."

I pulled my fingers out and growled out, "Ass up, Devlin."

She complied immediately.

I slid a condom on and grabbed her hips, pulling her to me, not that it took much effort, she was already arching her back, her ample ass perfectly on display. "Fuck, baby," I breathed out as I slid into her. Jesus, she felt incredible. "You're so tight."

She mewed and pushed back against me and I gave her ass a light tap. She hissed out and her walls contracted around me. I grinned. "You like that, apparently."

"You got another one in you?"

"I can slap your ass all day long, Devlin."

She chuckled. "I was talking about your boner, but I'll take that, too."

"That was all about you, baby," I said, pushing further into her. "I'm like the Energizer Bunny, I can go all night."

She gasped and arched up again. "Yes."

"You want harder?"

"Definitely," she rasped.

I slammed into her, keeping her anchored to the back of the sofa, but it wasn't giving me enough room to move, so I slid out of her and turned her to face me. "Bedroom."

She nodded, and I lifted her so she could wrap her legs around me before carrying her back to her bedroom. I dropped her gently on the bed, replaced the condom, and fisted myself as I pushed into her. Devlin whimpered with need as I hovered over her, sucking a nipple into my mouth and thrusting into her.

"More," she begged.

I grinned, kissing her gently, then buried myself deeper before rearing back and slamming into her over and over. I felt my sac tighten as an orgasm built, and tried to hold it at bay, but when her pussy contracted around me, I lost my self-control, exploding into her and grunting as she milked every ounce from me.

I allowed her to catch her breath and then kissed her once more, deeply before rolling onto my back, and Devlin settled her head onto my chest.

"How did you get the name Ropes?"

"It's a stupid story," I said dismissively.

"Come on, don't be like that. You promised you'd tell me."

"It's not that I don't want to tell you, it's just that you've built it up in your mind to be some big thing and it's not."

"Then, tell me," she said, slapping my chest.

"You smack my chest a lot, you know?"

"Do I?" she asked sheepishly. "I will confess that it's kind of my favorite part of your body, so I probably just can't keep my hands off it."

"Your favorite part huh?"

"Yes, now don't change the subject, *Ropes*. Spill now."

"Alright, but I'm warning you, it's a dumb story."

"I'll be the judge of that."

"I like to dress nice," I began.

"Nooooo, really?"

"Do you want to hear this or not?"

"I'm sorry," Devlin said and brought her lips to mine for a kiss. "I won't interrupt again, I promise."

"It's true, I grew up with money. My family is pretty well-off and I always grew up wearing high-quality clothes. When I moved out on my own, I lost my appetite for most of the so-called "finer things," but not clothes or jewelry."

"Jewelry?"

"Nothing too crazy. Just nice watches, the occasional gold chain, that kind of thing. No big deal as far as I was concerned. Well, it was a big deal to the guys I live with at the Sanctuary."

"How many of you live there?"

"Including my brother and me, usually about a dozen or so. Most of the officers and old-timers don't, but Sweet Pea and I had nowhere to go when we hooked up with the Saints, so we were more than happy to move in. I guess I've just never had a reason to leave."

"And the name?"

"One of the best and worst things about living in a house with a bunch of bikers is the constant tormenting of one another. It's how ninety-percent of club names are earned, and mine is no different."

"Please don't tell me this is an autoerotic asphyxiation story."

"Why do you keep assuming the story is sexual?"

"Sorry, shutting up."

"I came to breakfast one morning without a shirt on and Ringo, Wolf and a couple of the other older guys started calling me Mr. T and 2 Chainz because of the gold chains I was wearing. They kept it up all day, working every slang for necklace they could think of into their juvenile insults, until finally they'd resorted to simply calling me Ropes."

"That's a pretty stupid story," Devlin said, then broke into hysterical laughter.

I pounced on top of her and tickled her sides making her squeal and giggle uncontrollably while I rained down kisses on her neck.

"Stop, stop! Okay, you win, I'm sorry."

"You know, for being my muse, you're pretty mean to me,"

"What does it actually mean to 'be a muse'?" Devlin asked sweetly. "The job has to be more than just being an inspiration for something, right?"

"Mmm hmm."

"Is there a job description or something? Do I have official duties?" she asked playfully while she gently stroked my chest.

"In Greek mythology, the nine daughters of Zeus and Mnemosyne were the muses. They were tasked to inspire the great artists of Rome. But they did more than inspire artists. They compelled the art into being. The writers, poets, painters and musicians would go mad if they could not bring these creations to be."

"You think I'm a goddess?"

"As close a description as I'm able to come up with."

"And you *really* think I'm your Muse?"

"Do you want to know who I think you really are?" I asked.

"Who?" she asked, looking up at me.

"The woman I'm falling in love with."

"Please don't say shit like that," Devlin said, sitting up, grabbing my kutte to cover herself.

"Don't do that," I said stopping her. "Don't hide yourself when you're alone with me."

"Ropes—"

"And don't say that my feelings for you are shit. I'm falling in love with you Devlin whether you like it or not. In fact, I'm probably more than just falling—"

"Stop right there," Devlin said, scrambling to her feet and collecting her clothes. "This has all been really fun. You are a great guy, especially in bed, but I have to get out of here right now. In fact, I need to put an end to all of... .*this*," she said waving her free arm.

"What?"

"You know what I'm talking about, and you also know just as well as I do that things could never work between us."

"I do?" I asked with a chuckle. "That's odd, I don't recall thinking that at all. I thought we've been having a great time."

"We have, but really, what kind of future do you really see us having together? In your version of the story, do the struggling tattoo artist and biker/romance novelist ride off into the sunset together on a Harley?"

"Indian."

Devlin scrunched up her nose. "Who's Indian in this story?"

I laughed. "No, my bike. You said we'd ride off together on my Harley, but I ride an Indian Chief Dark Horse."

"I never said we'd be riding off on anything. The only one headed outta Dodge is me."

"So that's it?"

"Yes, I guess it is."

"Okay, then," I said, and began to dress.

"Really?"

"You sound surprised."

"I guess I just thought you'd be more upset after what you just said to me."

"I'm not happy about it, but I'm not going to stand here and beg for you to feel the same way about me that I do about you."

"Good."

"Great."

"We'll just get dressed and go our separate ways," she said in a tone that sounded more like she was convincing herself of her plan rather than informing me.

"I already know where I'm headed next," I said sliding on a boot.

"Headed next? It's late. Where are you going?"

"Not that it's any of your business, but after I fuck I'm usually starving, so I'm gonna go get some donuts."

Devlin's eyes widened. "Donuts?"

"The best imaginable," I replied.

"What donut shop is open at this hour?"

"None of them, but I know a guy."

"You have a donut guy?"

"I have *the* donut guy, but none of this information matters now because you and I are done," I said plainly as Devlin finished dressing. She was beautiful in ways that I didn't know a woman could be beautiful. There were a million little, ordinary things about her that turned me on, from the way her nostrils flared just a little when she laughed, to the shape of her lips. There was nothing about her that did not seem as if it were tailor-made just for me. The more I got to know her, the more I wanted to know her, and if she thought I was just going to let her walk out of my life now, she was even crazier than I'd hoped, but she didn't have to know that.

"I know we're done. I'm the one that said we're done, so we're… done," Devlin said matter-of-factly.

"Yup, super clear on that. So, I'm going for donuts, you want to come with me or what?"

"I thought you said you were clear?"

"I am. I'm also hungry and could easily destroy three of Omar's glazed twists right about now. I see no reason why you couldn't join me."

"But we just broke up, or whatever that was."

"So, we'll just be two friends getting donuts late at night."

Devlin's eyes narrowed. She stared at me as if I were a Jackson Pollock painting that she was trying to get a handle on.

She finally replied with, "Just donuts."

"Just donuts."

Devlin

WE PULLED UP to Top O' the Morning Donuts a little after two in the morning. I'd insisted on the two of us driving separately, not only because I wanted there to be clear boundaries between Ropes and me, but because I was also scared to death of motorcycles and never had any intention of getting on one as long as I lived.

As I slid out of my car and watched Ropes climb off his bike, I forced back tears. What was I thinking letting this guy go? Warding Ropes off before things got any more serious felt like the *right* thing to do, so why did I feel like complete shit?

It took more than a few convulsive swallows and a vivid imagining of fat old men mud wrestling to stop wishing he was riding me instead of his bike. Ropes walked to me and smiled. "You okay?"

No, sir, I'm not okay. I want you to rip my panties off and eat me out on the sidewalk in front of your friend's donut shop, which is extremely inconvenient for me considering I just dumped you.

"Yep."

"Why do you look like you just threw up in your mouth, then?"

Danny DiVito just pinned Hurly from Lost to a muddy mat, that's why.

"I have no idea," I lied. "I'm good."

He raised an eyebrow. "You sure?"

"Yep."

"Alrighty then, you ready to destroy some donuts?"

"Hells, yes, I am."

Hells yes? What the fuck, Devlin? Are we stuck in 1999?

I shook my head and followed him to the side entrance and Ropes quietly ushered me into the building. Ropes put a finger to his lips and we crept silently through the most wonderful smelling kitchen I'd ever encountered. As we made our way to the front of the shop I could see a slender man with salt and pepper hair sitting at one of the dining area tables, hunched over an old-school accounting ledger, scribbling away furiously with a pencil.

"Did someone here order an anchovy and pineapple pizza?"

The man at the ledger jumped in his seat and spun around before leaping to his feet to greet us.

"Dough Boy," he exclaimed cheerfully, as he pulled Ropes in for a bear hug.

"Dough Boy?" I snorted in surprise.

"That's what Omar has always called me. When I was a kid, I worked at Sparky's Pizza, which used to be right next door. If we were there late enough after closing, we could smell Omar baking his first batch of donuts. We'd bang on the common wall between us, and if Omar banged back we'd fire the oven back up and bake a large anchovy and pineapple pizza. In trade, Omar would give us two dozen donuts straight off the line. The Devil's Cut."

"And Dough Boy would always be the one to bring me my pie."

"Fucking anchovy and pineapple."

"Light cheese, and extra sauce," Omar added, wagging his finger. "Extra sauce is key."

"Good ol' Sparky's," Ropes said. "We had some good times there."

Omar scowled. "Now there's a fucking Jumpy Juice next door. All day long, women in yoga pants park their Priuses in my spaces," he said in a thick middle-eastern accent.

"You need me to talk to the owners?" Ropes asked, and the two men laughed.

"I'm just grumpy old man. But why talk about such things when we have beautiful lady in room?"

"Devlin, this is Omar," Ropes introduced us.

Omar smiled with his entire face as he greeted me. "It is so nice to have you in my brother's store. You are most welcome."

"Thank you so much. It smells amazing in here. Is your brother baking with you today?"

"Always," Omar said, gently patting his heart. "My brother Asim died when we were very young men in Sudan, but he is always right here with me."

"I'm so sorry," I said.

"It was Asim's dream to come to America. He had a crazy idea about selling coffee and donuts to Americans." Omar smiled and shrugged. "When he died, I left Sudan and came to America to fulfill my brother's dream."

"That is the sweetest thing I've ever heard," I said, as tears welled up.

"Perhaps," He looked around. "But now, there's giant green sign on every corner, and still only one Top O' the Morning Donuts." Omar laughed heartily.

"Your coffee is better than that corporate crap any day of the week," Ropes said. "And I've never had a better donut in my life."

"Speaking of donuts," Omar said, excitedly. "I've got a chocolate Bavarian cream with your name on it, little lady… if you like chocolate Bavarian cream, that is."

"You had me at Bavarian," I said.

"Oh, I *like* you." He dropped his head back and laughed. "I have fresh batch coming up. I'll go back to the kitchen and leave you two." Omar said.

"Corner booth okay?" Ropes asked.

"Always for you, anything," Omar replied, and disappeared.

"He's adorable," I said.

"Omar is the best."

"What did he think when Dough Boy became Biker Boy?"

"Omar was the one that introduced me to the Saints," Ropes said with a smile.

"Really?"

"Yeah. When I first got to town, I was just a kid. I didn't have a job or even a place to stay, so I applied at every place I could find but no one would hire me. I could hardly blame them. I was sixteen, looked like a ninety-nine-pound wet sack of turds, had no address, and zero work experience. The only guy that took me seriously was Dave Bracco, Breeder of Fine Hunting Dogs."

"Who?" I said with a laugh.

"Dave Bracco. He was the manager of Sparky's pizza. He gave me my first job and he became one of my best friends in the world."

"And he bred hunting dogs?"

Ropes smiled. "No, but according to him, the name Bracco is Italian and translated to 'Breeder of Fine Hunting Dogs.' He got a big kick out of this and had it printed on his business cards and everything."

"Even though he never actually bred hunting dogs?"

"Fine hunting dogs," Ropes corrected.

I smiled. "Sounds like a funny guy."

"He was a lunatic, told the corniest jokes, and was one of the best souls you ever could have met."

"Was?" I asked.

"He passed away when I was nineteen. He was murdered."

My hand covered my mouth. "Oh, my word, I'm so sorry."

"It's okay. It was a long time ago," Ropes said with a look in his eyes that told me that it may as well have been yesterday, but before I could find out more, Omar arrived back at our table with an assortment of freshly baked donuts on a tray.

"A little of everything, and a Bavarian cream for the lady," he said with a wink before noticing the wetness in my eyes.

Omar looked to Ropes for an explanation.

"I was just telling her about Dave Bracco," he said.

"Oh. Poor, poor David," Omar said, shaking his head. "Such a shameful thing to happen to such a good man."

"What happened?" I asked.

"The owner of Sparky's Pizza was a Russian mob guy named Rudy. He owned this whole building complex back then. Omar was the only one who owned his own business, and everything else in the complex was run by this scumbag.

"And I still had to kick up to that piece of shit," Omar said.

Ropes continued. "Apparently, one night, Dave saw Rudy do something that he shouldn't have, and it cost him his life."

"That's horrible. Did the police ever catch him?"

Omar and Ropes shared a look. "The matter was handled, justice was served," Ropes replied.

"How?"

"Omar was aware that the Burning Saints were known to help out business owners who were being hassled. After what happened to Dave, Omar was afraid for me, so he reached out to them, and the Saints took care of everything. Omar vouched for me, told Cutter I was a good kid, and the Saints took me in."

"That was good of you to look after him like that," I said.

"Dough Boy took care of me, so I took care of him," Omar said.

Ropes jumped in before Omar could say anything else. "And now Omar and the Burning Saints are business partners in the entire complex."

"Which is very good thing, because my idiot brother Asim left out the part about selling coffee and donuts in America where you go fucking broke." Omar's laugh broke the heaviness in the room.

"But, you're an artist, Omar," Ropes said.

"And now, thanks to you and the club, I can make art, and not starve to death," Omar said stepping back, palms up. "Please, while they are fresh,"

I took a bite of my donut and couldn't stop an orgasmic moan. "Oh my god, it's still so warm," I breathed out.

Ropes grinned. "Like nothing you've ever had before, right?"

"It melted in my mouth."

"I'm jealous," he said with a wink.

"Coffee," Omar exclaimed suddenly. "I must make coffee."

Before we could protest, he disappeared into the kitchen once more.

"I'll never get to sleep if I have one sip of coffee," I said, noticing an uneaten glazed twist sitting in front of Ropes. "Aren't you going to eat yours?" I asked.

"Maybe later," he said softly.

"But you'll miss all the warm gooey freshness," I replied.

"I'm not missing any of that," he said while looking into my eyes in a way that no man has ever done before. My stomach dropped, and my field of vision narrowed, the first two indications that I'm about to have a panic attack. My hand reflexively reached for Ropes. This was not normal behavior on my part. Typically, the last thing I'd want at a time like this would be physical contact with anyone, let alone a guy I was trying to break up with… if that was, in fact, what I was trying to do.

A look of concern washed over Ropes's face. "Baby are

you okay?"

Baby? Are you fucking kidding me?

A medium sized wave of terror hit me, and I felt my hands go cold and clammy. Obviously, Ropes did too, because he slid to my side of the booth and put his arms around me, pulling me in tight. My instincts told me to push him away and scream "Leave me the fuck alone," but my heart did not agree with this plan, so I remained frozen. Once again, unable to fight or flee. But, was I truly unable to run from this man? Was I truly frozen, or did I simply feel better when I was in Ropes's arms?

I burst into tears. "Please don't leave me."

"Leave you?" He chuckled. "If I recall, you're the one trying to give me the brush off and this was just supposed to be about donuts."

I looked up at him and his eyes met mine. "What if I want it to be more than just donuts?"

"I'll ask Omar if he has sprinkles."

I smacked Ropes's chest and another wave of emotion hit me. It was only then I realized that I was not having an anxiety attack, but that I was falling in love.

Ropes looked deeply into my puffy eyes. "Devlin, I'm not going anywhere. I think I've made myself very clear about how I feel about you, and I think you have the same feelings for me too, but are afraid to admit it, which is totally okay. So, when you want to be with me, I'll be here, and if you need me to back off, I can do that as well."

"I don't want you to back off," I admitted.

"Good, because I don't want to. I want to be 'all in' with you."

"But why? You barely know me."

Ropes pulled back to look directly at me. "Baby, I've known you since the second I first saw you. The day you walked into Sally Anne's my entire life changed. You not only inspired a new story in my head, but you put deep hooks into my heart. I don't know how, but you did. All I'm asking for, is a chance to get to know each other, the real you and me. I don't want to play games and bullshit around with you Devlin. I'm not interested in "dating" you, I just want to be with you. Simple as that."

"Oh, sure. Real simple," I replied, shoving the last bite of my second donut in my mouth.

"Why can't it be? We're two young, single people, living in Portland, trying to find a way to make a living with our art."

I choked on the oversized bite. "I think you forgot a few details."

"Not any important ones," he replied, much to my surprise.

"Your club isn't important?"

"Not as it pertains to us."

"I find that hard—" I shook my head. "No, impossible to believe."

"My ability to prioritize and compartmentalize may surprise you."

I was intrigued. "Oh?" I asked casually as I eyed another sugary ring of sin.

Just then, Omar returned with a carafe and a large pink box tied up with twine.

"Coffee for you and donuts for the club."

"Thank you so much, Omar," Ropes said as he rose to his feet. "Would it be possible to get those coffees to go?"

"Of course, my friend, I'll get cups for you. But no straws, the hipsters will throw rocks at my store if I give you straws," Omar said and left us with the box.

Ropes smiled wide and extended his hand. "Come on, there's one more place I want to show you."

"Isn't there some sort of rule about never going to a third location?" I teased as I stood.

"I think that only pertains to places that serve alcohol. As you can see, my weakness is baked goods."

"You'd never know it by your abs," I said, my hand going to his body as I leaned in for a kiss.

"Thank you," Ropes said, reaching for his donut and quickly devouring half of it in a single bite.

I laughed. "What was that all about?"

"I wanted this donut to be the second sweetest thing on my lips tonight."

The line was corny, sappy, and normally something I'd throat punch a guy for saying. At that moment, however, all I wanted to do was to marry Ropes, move to a cabin in the woods, and bear him twelve children.

TEN

BURNING SAINTS

Ropes

WE SAID OUR goodbyes to Omar and walked out to Devlin's VW Thing.

"Let's put the coffee and donuts in your car, and you can ride with me, it's not very far."

"What? On *that*?" Devlin said, pointing to my bike.

"Sure," I laughed. "What else?"

"Oh, I don't know? How about a car, or bus, or a freaking pogo stick? Anything but one of those rolling coffins."

"I can see you have strong feelings about motorcycles."

"I'll be more than happy to follow you," she said taking the coffee and donuts from my hands.

I smiled. "We can ride another time then."

"Yes, when the Browns win the Superbowl," she said

and climbed into her car.

I fired up my bike and Devlin followed me the two short miles to our destination, a newly built, high-end apartment complex. I directed Devlin to a side street and had her park next to me in a loading zone.

"Are you sure we're okay here?"

"It's alright." I assured her. "We won't be long."

Devlin got out of the car and joined me as I stood in front of the massive structure.

"What are we looking at?" she asked, shivering from the cold.

I put my arm around her and pulled her in tight. "This is where I lived when I first came to Portland."

"Nice place. Looks a little new, though," she said, surprised.

"No, this building wasn't here then, and if it was, I wouldn't have been able to afford the rent in the janitor's closet. I lived in the empty field that was here before all of this." I motioned to the surroundings, which were rich with signs of recent development.

"Why were you living in a field? I thought you had money?"

"My family has money, and I don't want anything to do with my family, so I came here, alone, with nothing."

"Why did you run away?"

"Lots of reasons, but the final straw was when my little brother was abused, and my father refused to do anything about it."

"Why?"

"Because, the man who abused my brother was our uncle, my father's brother."

"Your dad didn't do anything?" she asked. "What about your mother? Didn't someone report your uncle to the police?"

"Devlin, I'm going to tell you something that only a few people know." I turned to face her. "My real name is Spencer Kimble."

Devlin stared at me, her eyes narrowing in concentration,

before she shook her head as if to say "sorry, not ringing any bells."

"Kimble... as in Kimble and Hill," I further clarified, and a look of shock came over her face.

"Are you kidding me? Kimble and Hill is one of the biggest corporations in the country, and you're telling me that you're related to them?"

"Not just related. My great grandfather was Albert Kimble, co-founder of the company, and my grandfather made the company what it is today."

"You said your family had money, not your family was made of money itself."

"You can see why I don't normally share this information with people."

Devlin nodded.

"I went to private schools growing up. I had nannies, tutors, and every indulgence I could want. Groomed my entire life to be the next in line to run the company."

"And you left all of that behind?" she asked.

"My uncle raped my little brother and no one in my family did a single thing to help him. Everyone just wanted everything to be quietly swept under the rug. Nothing that could sully the family name or affect the bottom line would be permitted. My father knew that a scandal like that would rock the boardroom, and that the company stock would tumble."

"So, you just took off for Portland, all by yourself?"

"Not exactly." I paused, deciding exactly how much I should tell Devlin about this part of the story. I wanted to be completely open and honest with her about who I was, but I didn't want to burden her with details that might be upsetting or compromise her. On the other hand, my life wasn't always pretty. In fact, it was usually pretty fucking messy. If Devlin wanted to be a part of it, she'd need to know the score, so I decided to give her the unredacted version of the events.

"If I tell you all about my past, there's no going back for me," I said.

Her brow furrowed as she asked, "What do you mean?"

"I'm telling you every secret I have, Devlin. Shit that could cost me my freedom, or even my life. I'm not just giving you information about who I am, I'm putting my entire heart in your hands. Outside of my brother, I've never trusted anyone with what I'm about to tell you."

Devlin pulled me in for a long kiss and it took every ounce of my composure not to fuck her up against the building.

"I don't know what to say," she whispered, breaking the kiss.

"It's okay, just listen," I said, taking a deep breath. "When my brother told me what my uncle had done to him, I flipped out. I went straight to my dad who assured me that he would handle it, which of course he did by telling my brother to keep his mouth shut. Our mother died when I was seven and my brother, Charlie, was three years old. I only have a handful of memories of my mother, but he doesn't have any. Only a box of photos. My father and uncle were the only family we had, and now my brother had been betrayed by both. There was no way in hell I was going to let this stand, so a few days later I snuck into my father's office, logged into his computer and sent an email to everyone in his address book that contained sensitive information regarding a secret corporate merger he'd been working on for six months. The leak cost him millions."

She frowned. "Did he find out that you were the one who'd done it?"

"Not until I told him."

"You admitted to it?" she asked, surprised.

"The very next morning I came down stairs to find my father in a panic. He was in his home office, screaming to his assistant on the phone. He'd obviously figured out that he'd been hacked, and the shit was hitting the fan. I came in to let him know that I had a present for him. It wasn't his birthday, so he was understandably confused, but I convinced him to take a few minutes to indulge me."

Devlin's eye widened. "What did you have for him?"

"You know, some people like to hear a story and not just

jump to the end."

"So, I've been told," she said, giving me the universal hurry it up hand signal.

"I handed my father a small tin box with a bow on it. It was one of those breath mint tins, but that's not what was inside."

"What was inside?"

"Eight of my uncle's teeth," I replied.

Devlin gasped, but said nothing.

"Do you want me to go on?" I asked.

She nodded.

"After I'd hacked my father's email, I paid a visit to my uncle's estate. He was surprised to see me but opened the gate when I showed up. He had no reason not to. He didn't know that my brother had said anything to me about the abuse, or what I had planned for him. I told him I was there so late because I'd had a fight with my dad and was hoping I could talk to him about it. My uncle lived alone, so I knew we'd have privacy. He invited me in and asked if I wanted anything to drink. I asked him for a coke and the moment he returned from the kitchen, I confronted him about Charlie's accusations. You know what the really fucked up thing was?"

"What?"

"He didn't deny it. Didn't even try to explain it away. Nothing. He just said that it was consensual, that Charlie wanted it as much as he did. He said that Charlie needed to acknowledge that fact. I started to rage inside but didn't completely lose it until he laughed."

Devlin blinked back tears.

"Like a fucking maniac, the man laughed at the trauma he'd just caused my brother, so I hit him over the head with a ten-inch length of pipe I had hidden in my coat. He dropped to the floor and I was right on top of him. With every blow I let him know exactly why I was there, to deliver justice for my brother. When I was done with him, he was barely breathing, barely human. I saw a bunch of his teeth laying in a pool of blood and collected them carefully one-by-one."

"Why?"

"I took the tin full of teeth when I left my father's office and I mailed them to my uncle every year on the anniversary of that day."

"What for?"

"To remind him that I' be watching. To remind that sick fucker to be on his best behavior. Not that he had much of a choice. The beating left him in a wheelchair for the rest of his life, unable to walk, speak properly, or ever get it up again. I took from him what he took from my brother, the ability to live a normal life ever again."

Devlin blinked back tears. "But you gave up your life too."

"That's true, and I'd do it all again for my brother. I left that night and have never spoken to my father since. He paid off the papers to say that my uncle had been in a terrible car accident."

"What about your brother?"

"I couldn't take Charlie with me. Not until I was set up somewhere. I didn't have any money or a place to stay. He was only twelve and even greener than I was. It was tough enough for me out here on the streets, he wouldn't have lasted the first week. It would take a few years for me to get him out here."

"And your uncle?"

"He killed himself after tooth number six showed up. I was never able to mail him the last two. I still keep them as a reminder, and I've been in the habit of reminding bad people to be good via this method ever since." I pulled out an empty envelop and handed it to Devlin.

She glanced at the top of it. "Is this addressed to the same Troy who tried to attack me?"

"That's right," I said and removed Troy's teeth from my kutte pocket and took the envelope from Devlin. "He's never going to hurt you again. I promise that," I said, sliding the teeth into the envelope before sealing it. "I've always mailed these special packages from this particular mailbox, the one closest to this spot." I pulled the handle on the blue mailbox and dropped the envelope inside.

* * *

Devlin

Normal people would probably turn tail and run far away from a man so violent. Normal people would also not excuse the behavior of that man, regardless of the reasons.

But I was no longer normal. Hadn't been for a long, long time. And I was still trying to heal.

Gentle fingers on my cheek had me focusing back on Ropes as he lifted my chin. "I need to know what you're thinking, baby."

I licked my lips. "I was just thinking that my fucked-up life kind of matches your fucked-up life to a T."

"Yeah?"

I nodded. "I was twenty-two, just out of art school, ready to start taking on the world when I met Tripp."

"Tripp is a douche name."

"Tripp was a douche," I confirmed. "But I fell hard. He was very pretty, had a lot of money, and made me feel special. I'd never had that before. I was always the gangly, freckled redhead most kids made fun of, but he told me how beautiful I was and made me feel like I actually was."

"You are."

I shook my head. "You have to stop interrupting me, or I'll never get through this."

He pulled me against him and stroked my back. "Sorry. Continue."

"One night, he took me to a party where his 'friends' were. He offered me up to one of them and I was like, hell no, and told him exactly what I thought of him. I might have been insecure, but I wasn't about to let him pass me around. He apologized profusely, promised he'd never ask again... then handed me a drink. Like a lamb to the slaughter, I drank it." I closed my eyes tight, trying to force down the panic I felt at telling Ropes my story.

"I've got you, Devlin. No one will ever hurt you again."

"I woke up in a storage container, chained to the wall with six other girls of varying ages. My body screamed in pain, but the abject terror I felt seemed to mask it. I have no idea how long we were in the container, but we arrived at some flophouse and were thrown into different rooms and guarded night and day. I came to find out it was some meth house in Savannah, Georgia, and we joined seven other girls. There was a little girl named Molly. I think she was ten." I burrowed into Ropes's chest and forced back tears. "They were auctioning her off to the highest bidder. The rest of us were used by whoever was there at the time, or those men willing to come into the slums to partake. They would shoot us up with heroin to keep us willing and quiet, but I got too sick from the drugs, so they would gag me, so my screams wouldn't be heard."

Ropes's body locked as he hissed out, "Jesus fuckin' Christ."

"Don't use the Lord's name in vain, Ropes. Please," I begged.

"Sorry, baby. I'll be better."

"I was there for over a month. One of the girls, Scarlett, had made herself Molly's protector and got beaten a lot, but she was one of the lucky ones. Her brother had been looking for her and ended up finding all of us as well. His wife used to be a nun and organized a plan with the FBI to keep us all hidden."

"How?"

"We were hidden in plain sight, dressed as nuns in an Abbey in Beaverton."

"You're kidding me."

"All true. In fact, we came back to Portland, dressed as nuns until it was safe for us to come out of hiding."

"Safe according to who?" Ropes asked, a look of concern etched deeply into his face.

"The FBI," I assured him. "Don't worry, the people that did this to us are all in Federal Prison or were killed by their employers. We worked with the FBI for months before the case was closed."

"That explains the small footprint," Ropes said quietly.

"What's that?" I asked.

"Promise you won't get mad, but I had a friend of mine run a background check on you."

"A background check?"

"I needed to know if I could trust you and was looking for any red flags."

I wanted to be mad or at least hurt, but I couldn't be. I'd have done the exact same thing if I had a "background check guy" at my disposal.

"I assume you didn't find anything interesting." I said sarcastically.

"Oddly enough, no." Ropes said plainly.

"What do you mean oddly enough?"

"Come on now. I don't think I'm an asshole for expecting you to have at least a few marks on your permanent record."

"Did you find anything during your little search?"

"No, but that doesn't tell the whole story does it?"

"What are you saying?"

"That I would have expected a rebel like you to have left a few tracks on the streets, but I guess I was wrong...unless."

"Unless what?"

"Unless your friends at the FBI cleared up your record in exchange for your cooperation in a Federal investigation."

"Let's just say it wasn't only the nuns that helped absolve me of my sins."

"What about your family? Where were they during all of this?"

"My father left when I was two years old and died when I was twelve. My mom was in and out of jail and mental institutions most my life. I honestly don't know where she is now, if she's even alive, and I don't want to."

"I understand. I'm sorry," Ropes said softly.

"It's okay. Being taken was the worst thing that had ever happened to me, but it led me to the sisters and they changed my life."

"So, that's why you can't handle blasphemy."

I nodded. "The sisters are the only reason I'm standing in front of you now. Those women were so amazing. We were all in various states of trauma and they loved us unconditionally. I never felt judged by them, not once. And Sadie, she was the one who used to be a nun, is the nicest person you'll ever meet. So is her husband, Ryder. He let me work at his bar, as a barback. It's also where I started meeting my first tattoo clientele."

"Ryder," he mused. "Does he own the Brass Frog?"

"Yes. Do you know him?"

"Not well, but he runs with the Dogs, so we occasionally see each other."

"He runs with dogs? Is this another Dave Bracco joke?"

Ropes laughed. "The Dogs of Fire MC. They're a local club that we're... friendly with... more or less," he explained.

"I know their club," I said. "Some of their guys have work done at one of the shops I freelance out of."

"Makes sense," Ropes said. "Cricket knows Ryder's woman pretty well, too, I think. Sadie's cool. We all like her."

"She's amazing," I agreed. "We get together for girls' night on occasion. She's so funny when she's tipsy and Ryder's super protective, which makes her get all bossy with him. It's actually kind of hilarious."

"Yeah?"

I nodded and smiled up at him. "Something about bringing an alpha man to his knees... it's invigorating."

He raised an eyebrow. "Do you still have your nun costume?"

I groaned. "It's not a costume, it's a sacred garment."

"Okay, so I take it, you won't wear it for me with nothing underneath, so I can fuck you in it sometime?"

I bit back a chuckle. "You are the worst."

He smiled, stroking my cheek before kissing me gently. "I'm sorry you had to deal with that shit, baby. You ever need anything from me, I'm here."

"I know. It's probably why I pushed you away," I admitted. "Pretty… with money… making me feel special."

"I'm nothing like this Tripp shithead."

"I know," I rushed to say. "I'm learning to trust you, and for what it's worth, you've gained it more than most."

"I appreciate that."

I wrapped my arms around him and squeezed.

We stood like this, in the middle of a loading dock, for several minutes until it was time to get moving. I slid into Ben and Ropes climbed onto his bike and we took off, headed back to my place where he stayed until I woke him the next morning.

ELEVEN

BURNING SAINTS

Ropes

T HE PAST WEEK with Devlin had kept my mind completely off club business, not that there was much actual business to speak of these days. Minus had made it very clear that the club was set on cash for the moment, but our reserves wouldn't last forever. The number one priority on the street was paving new avenues of revenue.

There was a knock at my door followed by, "You awake, shithead?"

"Come on in," I called back, and my little brother, Sweet Pea, entered my cramped bedroom. The space was nothing more than a converted utility room, but it was private. Growing up, my brother and I always had our own rooms, and to this day, I found it next to impossible to cohabitate with any-one.

"Wolf wants us wheels-up in five minutes."

"Why so fucking early?"

"I dunno, but he's in a shit mood, so I'd hop to it, big bro."

Wolf was always in a bad mood these days. The new world order was seriously cramping his style and I wasn't sure he'd be able to successfully navigate the club's transition over to the ninety-nine percenters.

"Hand me my boots, will you? They're right behind you."

Pea did so before asking, "Where you been all week?"

"I've been around. Had some shit to take care of," I said dismissively.

"Not what I heard," he replied with as much of a smile as he ever dared to crack.

"Oh, pray tell, little brother. What exactly did your big-ass ears hear?"

"Fuck you," he snapped back. "My ears aren't big. I have mom's ears."

I slid my boots on, stood up and grabbed my keys. "C'mon, if Wolf is on the rag, I don't want to give him a reason to bitch at us."

Sweet Pea screwed up his face. "Us? What the fuck are you talking about. Wolf likes *me*."

"Why wouldn't he, teacher's pet?"

"Fuck you," he replied without showing a trace of actual annoyance. My brother ran as cool as they came. Nothing rattled him. He was the bravest person I knew, but I worried about his devotion to our road captain, Wolf, who was clear-ly at odds with the President. I was afraid that if lines were drawn, little brother might be torn as to which side to stand on.

"Whatever your little sewing circle bitches told you is bullshit. I've been running errands and taking care of some personal shit, and by personal, I mean that it's nobody's godda… fucking business." I corrected myself mid-swear for

Devlin's sake, although she wasn't there.

"I heard you were hanging out at the mall with that hot redhead from Sally Anne's like some fuckin' teenager."

I had no idea who'd seen Devlin and me together, but I did not like being the topic of gossip. "Who the fuck told you that?"

"The Peckers said they saw you there last night, making out by that bookstore you like. When they mentioned that place, I knew it had to be you. Besides, a smokin' hot tatted-up redhead and a biker tend to stand out in a place like that, dontcha think?"

"Sure, so what the fuck were the Peckers doing there?" I asked.

"How the hell should I know? With those morons? Glow-in-the-dark golf and Hotdog on a Stick if I had to make a guess."

Big Pecker and Little Pecker were club prospects who'd been around for a while, who'd like have been patched in already if not for all the recent transitional drama. Minus felt that the club was in serious need of new blood. Guys who were free from the baggage of the past. Young guys who were able to find ways of earning within the new age. I agreed with Minus's philosophy but was unsure about the Peckers. They both seemed eager and followed instructions, but something about them gave me pause, although I'd never been able to pinpoint what it was. One thing was for certain, I'd have to see a hell of a lot more from them before I cast my vote for giving them patches and official names.

"Tell those two to mind their own fucking business," I said, opening the door out to the hallway, before stopping and adding, "No, wait. Forget that. I'll tell them myself."

Sweet Pea and I made our way to the Sanctuary's great hall where Wolf, Doozer, and Socks were waiting.

"'Bout fuckin' time. You finished putting on your mascara?" Wolf growled through his scraggly beard.

"Haven't had your coffee enema yet this morning, Boss?" I asked.

"Just for that, you're buying today."

The five of us rode out to Flick's Beanery, which was part of a small chain of coffee places in the area. Just about everyone in the Pacific Northwest, from the most hard-core biker to the corporate heavy hitters, was in the throes of a coffee addiction, but Wolf was a full-blown, black tar caffeine junkie. We'd stop for a fix three times a day at minimum.

While slamming down triple shot espressos, Wolf ran down our plans for the day, which included stopping by Sally Anne's, picking up two kegs of beer, and delivering them to Portland State University. The club was hosting a party for some of the young up-and-comers that Minus was betting would have serious political juice within the years to come. Minus was laying the groundwork for a new era of the Burning Saints. A sustainable future that would keep the club and all its members alive.

Wolf made no attempt to hide his disdain for the task. "Minus wants us to go play wet nurse to a bunch of privileged snot-nosed white boys."

"You're white, too," I replied with a laugh.

"Yeah, but I'm not a white-boy. There's a big fuckin' difference."

"If you say so, Boss."

"Good fuckin' answer."

"What does that make Ropes, then?" Doozer asked.

"He's the worst," Wolf replied. "He's a fuckin' pretty boy."

"Any time you want some beauty tips, you just let me know, Wolf."

"How 'bout I just make that face of yours a little less pretty."

"I know a guy who's got some gloves," I replied to raised eyebrows all around.

"Who needs gloves?" Wolf replied.

We were referring to Clutch's newly opened boxing gym. Our Sergeant at Arms was the first to get a legitimate business up and running, post Minus taking office, and it was an instant hit in the community. In fact, the club was already sponsoring several young fighters from the neighborhood. Wolf clearly had something a little less civilized in mind.

"Ding, ding!" I said with a smile, signifying the end of the round, my hands up in mock surrender. Wolf was my Captain, and I knew better than to cross the line too far, and although he didn't intimidate me, he was a man to be feared and respected.

Wolf looked at me but pointed at Sweet Pea. "You know, you should learn to be more like your brother, and keep your mouth fuckin' shut."

Pea simply shrugged.

"See what I mean? Now, let's get the fuck outta here," Wolf said, and we headed out to the parking lot, where the Peckers were waiting with a pickup truck.

"Minus wants full patches to represent at this frat party, so Doozer, you and Socks take the truck to Sally Anne's to pick up the kegs and deliver them. The Peckers can ride your bikes back to the Sanctuary," Wolf directed.

"Pea and I can do it," I said, my brother's head snapping to mine in surprise.

"Why?" Wolf asked.

"I've got some shit at the Sanctuary that I need to take to the dump and I could use the truck." This was bullshit. I was really hoping that Devlin would be at Sally Anne's. The grunt work would all be worth it if I could see her for a few minutes.

"Fine, whatever," Wolf grumbled. "Ropes and Sweet Pea can take care of the refreshments for Minus's little tea party and you two can come with me." He motioned to Doozer and Socks.

I walked over to the Peckers and handed Little Pecker the keys to my bike. He was a little smaller than me, but closer to my build than the massive Big Pecker.

"If she comes back with a single scratch, I'll break both of your thumbs," I said to him before turning to Big Pecker and adding, "Oh, one more thing. I heard you guys saw me at the mall this weekend."

Big Pecker smiled wide, giving me a beautiful target. My right hand connected perfectly with his pearly white grill and he staggered back as blood began to pour from the holes where his two front teeth had previously been.

"Whathefuckman?" Big pecker slurred as the rest of my brothers stood by, just as stunned as he was.

"If I ever hear about either of you running your mouth about me or my business again, I'll not only make sure you're out of this club, but off the face of this fucking planet. You got that?"

Sweet Pea handed big Pecker his keys and a rag. "Don't get blood all over my bike," was all he said, and we headed towards the truck.

* * *

Devlin

"Fucking fuckity fuck!" I yelped as I hopped up and down on my right foot. The pain in my left foot started at my little toe and shot all the way up to my knee. I gathered up my courage and looked down, only to see my fears realized. Rather than point north, the pinky toe on my left foot was pointing due west. I fought back the urge to vomit and found a seat before I passed out.

I'd uncharacteristically overslept and was running way behind schedule this morning. I was attempting to towel dry my hair and walk at the same time when instead of going home, my left little piggy went into the corner of my bedroom dresser. I was already late for a job that didn't have health coverage, so this was the absolute last thing in the world I needed. Not to mention the normal dread I felt any time my schedule was fucked with. Should I call an ambulance? Try to straighten my toe back out myself? The last thought made me want to hurl again so I quickly put it out of my mind.

I picked up the phone and called Ropes.

* * *

Ropes

Sweet Pea turned to me from the passenger seat. "You wanna tell me what the fuck just happened?" Before I could respond, my phone buzzed. It was Devlin.

"Give me a sec," I said. I stepped away from the truck and took the call. "Hey there, Cherry, you miss me already?" I joked.

"I need you... to come and take... me to a... doctor," Devlin said in between sobs, and my blood ran cold. I imagined her lying on the floor, in a pool of blood with Troy standing over her.

"What happened? Do you need me to call 9-1-1?"

"No," she said, now sounding a little calmer. "I broke my toe."

"*You broke your toe*? Jesus, Devlin. You gave me a fucking heart attack."

"Don't use the... Lord's name... in vain," she said.

"I'll be right there," I said, and hung up before climbing into the truck.

"What the fuck was that all about?" Sweet Pea asked as soon as I got behind the wheel.

"That was Devlin. She broke a toe so I'm gonna take her to the clinic."

"I wasn't talking about the phone call. I meant you cold cocking the prospect just now."

"The Peckers were out of line for talking about my business to you," I snapped.

"Maybe so, but that was a bit fuckin' much, bro. That's not all, either."

"What?"

"I didn't say shit earlier, but from the looks of your knuckles and nose, it looks like you've been fighting lately.

"It's not what you think," I said.

"I don't give a shit what it is, but if Minus hears that

97

you've been earning by collecting he's gonna be pissed."

I nervously glanced down at my kutte pocket.

"Oh, shit. No." Sweet Pea shook his head. "He's gonna lose his shit if he finds out the tooth fairy is back in business."

"This wasn't about collecting," I said.

"You knock people's teeth out and mail them back just for the fucking fun of it now?"

"No, Pea. This was personal. I was helping a friend out."

"This is all about her isn't it?" my brother replied in a far more animated fashion than he was typically known for.

"Let's get the fuck out here," I said and drove off.

TWELVE

BURNING SAINTS

Devlin

THE MOMENT I hung up the phone I felt like an idiot.

"Why did I call him?" I questioned out loud to
no one.

"Because he's your boyfriend," no one replied.

"He's *not* my boyfriend," I argued.

*"Then what is he? He told you he loves you, and it tem-
porarily freaked you out?"*

"First of all, he didn't say he loved me. He said he's falling in love with me."

"Same thing."

"No, it's not. And secondly, I clearly *am* losing it, because I'm arguing out loud to *absolutely no one*!"

I violently shook my fists to the sky and the movement caused pain to shoot up my leg. I covered my mouth to muffle a scream of agony. I'd endured hours of tattoo work, all over different parts of my body, but had never felt physical pain like this before. I needed ice, or better yet something to pour over ice. I stood up slowly and carefully, using the back of a suspect looking Ikea dining room chair to keep the weight off my leg. I then scooted the chair with me as I moved, using it as a giant crutch. It was slow going, and I probably looked like an insane person, but I had a stocked liquor cabinet, and something in there was gonna take the edge off this mortal injury.

I was almost to the far side of the kitchen when I heard three loud thumps on my front door, followed by Ropes's booming voice in the distance. "Devlin, open up, it's me!"

"Hold on!" I called out, but he obviously couldn't hear me, not to mention the act of yelling caused my foot to burn as if it were being stabbed with a hot fireplace poker.

"Devlin, can you hear me? The door's locked."

I scooted my chair/crutch around and tried to make my way to the door as quickly as possible.

I could hear the anxiety in Ropes's voice rise as I hobbled and moaned. "Devlin, baby! Are you okay? You're scaring me now. I'm gonna break the door down if you don't answer."

"Ropes, don't you dare!" I cried as I scooted as fast as my busted-ass little piggy could wee wee wee.

Just then, my door splintered into a million pieces and Ropes rushed in to find me in the middle of my living room, in my bathrobe, being supported by a Jokkmokk chair.

"What the hell happened? Why didn't you answer me?" he demanded, looking about as stunned as I was.

The only reply I could muster was, "My door...my toe...ow," and then burst into tears. Ropes scooped me up in his arms and spoke to Sweet Pea, a Saint I recognized from the bar.

"I'm gonna take her to Eldie's clinic. You stay here and watch the place. I'll call you in a little while and let you know what's going on."

"What the hell am I supposed to say to Wolf?" Sweet Pea asked.

"Damnit, Wolf," Ropes hissed. "Call a recruit to come fix this door and then you go pick up the keg from Sally Anne's and take it to the frat party."

"Sally Anne's!" I hissed. "Shit, I forgot to call her and tell her I'm gonna be late."

"Late nothing, you're gonna be off this foot for the rest of the day at least. Come on, you can call her from the car. We need to take your Thing."

"No one drives Ben but me," I protested.

"Okay, we'll wait for an Uber then. One should be here in no less than ten minutes this time of day. Shall I set you down here or outside on the curb?"

"Fine, the keys are in my purse," I said, motioning to my bag.

The other man handed it to me with a smile and Ropes said, "Devlin, you know my my little brother, Sweet Pea, right?"

I craned my neck up... and up some more. "Little brother?"

"Yeah, yeah, I know. He takes after our mother's side of the family. Apparently, they were all giant Vikings or something."

"It's very nice to meet you, Sweet Pea," I said with a slight wave. "If you'll excuse me, I need morphine now."

Sweet Pea gave me a tight-lipped smile and a nod and Ropes carried me down to Ben, and carefully placed me inside.

"Where are we going?" I asked as Ropes buckled me in.

"I'm taking you to Eldie's clinic."

"Who's Eldie?"

"She *was* our club's official/unofficial doctor for years. Someone we could always go to if we needed patching up, no questions asked, but now she's that and a lot more."

"How so?"

"She's also Clutch's old lady."

"Is she the gorgeous brunette I see him with at the bar sometimes?"

"No," Ropes said with a whisper. "That's Yolanda, one of his mistresses."

"What?" I gasped, shocked at what I was hearing. "Seriously?"

Ropes burst into laughter, "No, I'm totally kidding."

"You jerk," I said, slapping his arm, causing another twinge of pain. "Ow, my toe."

"Sorry, baby. Try to stay still."

"Please don't tell me Clutch is a dog. I've always gotten a good vibe from him when he's been in Sally Anne's."

"Been in Sally Anne's what?"

"Ow!" I howled in laughter and pain simultaneously.

"I'm sorry, I can't help myself," Ropes said, biting his knuckles.

"I set myself up for that one," I said wincing through the pain.

"I won't tease you anymore, I promise. And you can rest assured that Clutch's loyalty knows no bounds, especially when it comes to Eldie."

As Ropes drove us toward the clinic, despite the pain I was in, I was oddly at peace. In fact, it occurred to me that I couldn't remember the last time I'd felt a peace quite like this.

I called Sally Anne and let her know what was going on, and she assured me not to worry and that she'd find someone to cover any shifts necessary. After a big sigh of relief that my job was secure, and a short drive, we reached the clinic and Ropes carried me inside.

The receptionist smirked, raised an eyebrow at Ropes and simply said, "Exam room in the back. Katie's helping." Ropes nodded and took me through the waiting area, to the end of a hallway. I had no idea who Katie was, but if she gave me morphine, she'd be my best friend. Ropes carefully opened a plain, white door and carried me over the threshold like a bride.

Our eyes met as we stepped inside, and my insides turned

to goo. Straight up girlie goo. Purple with flecks of glitter in it. I hated myself for falling for this guy, but that was exactly what was happening. There was no way I could get away with lying to myself, so why spend energy I didn't have trying?

"There's a lamp. Watch your head," he said sweetly as he set me on the paper-clad exam table.

"I think I'm falling in love with you," I blurted out. Before I could even think about regretting it, Ropes's lips were on mine, tenderly but intensely. My head rested back against the small pillow and his hands went to the side of my face. I moaned in delight, momentarily forgetting about the pain in my foot, until the exam room door opened.

"Oh," a female voice said as she entered. "Sorry."

Ropes chuckled. "It's all good. Katie, this is Devlin."

Katie shook my hand with a sweet smile.

"Katie's brother, Flea, is a brother with the Dogs of Fire. She's helpin' Eldie out for a few months."

Katie nodded. "I'm a glutton for punishment and thought, 'hey, Katie, you don't have enough on your plate, how about you go back to school and be a nurse practioner?' You know, because RN just wasn't enough for me."

"I think it's admirable," I said, even though my foot felt like it was going to explode.

She grabbed a blood pressure cuff and secured it to my arm. "I'm just lucky to know a lot of rough and ready bikers who tend to get hurt so much, my friend offered me an intern position of sorts. Eldie's amazing."

The subject of our conversation stepped into the room just as Ropes kissed me again.

"So, *this* is happening, then?" She pointed quickly back and forth between the two of us.

"Hey, Eldie. How are you?" Ropes said sheepishly, now standing up straight. I think he was even blushing. "Devlin and I were just... this is all pretty new... and no one in the club..."

"Your secret's safe with me," Eldie said with a smile as she mimed zipping her lips and tossing the key over her shoulder.

Eldie turned her attention to me. "Hi, I'm Doctor Gardner," she said extending a hand. "You can call me Gina... or Eldie. That's what all the club guys call me."

From my current position, I could now see she was pregnant.

"Nice to meet you, I'm Devlin."

"You work at Sally Anne's place, right?"

I furrowed my brow. "I'm supposed to be there right now."

"So, what, besides an obvious case of love sickness, brings you to my clinic today?"

Now *I* was blushing. Big time. "I stubbed my toe on my dresser and I think it's broken," I said, and Ropes stepped out of the way to reveal the carnage.

"Oh my," she replied at the sight of my left foot, which had now swollen to Mickey Mouse proportions, not to mention the toe looked like it was trying to escape from my foot. "We don't need an x-ray to see that's a broken toe. Let me get you a wheelchair and Katie and I'll take you back to the x-ray machine. Ropes, why don't you make yourself a cup of coffee and say hi to Maggie? I'm sure she has some paperwork that she'd appreciate being distracted from."

Ropes gave Doctor Gardner a smile and tipped an imaginary hat to the two of us before backing out of the room.

"You all set on birth control?" she asked as soon as Ropes was gone. "Because I'm betting that boy could get a woman pregnant just by looking at her."

"I'm good, Doc... ah, Eldie," I said with a nervous laugh. "How did you get your name?"

"L.D. is short for lady doctor," she said raising an eyebrow.

"And the man that called you that is still alive?"

"Actually, no. He's not." Eldie said.

"Oh, my God. I'm sorry. I was trying to make a joke," I said, feeling the heat of embarrassment creep up the back of my neck.

"It's okay," Elie whispered, leaning in close. "They'll

never find Red Dog's body and he'll never call me "Lady Doctor" again."

"You've definitely been hanging around bikers," I said, smiling.

"They started hanging around me first," she said.

"And I can see why," I replied.

I filled out some insurance paperwork and was administered valium and Vicodin.

"So, you and Ropes, huh?" Eldie asked as we finished up.

I giggled. "Do we share doctor/patient privilege here?"

"Better," she said in a more serious tone. "We share club chick privilege. Devlin, if you're with a Saint, nothing you say will ever leave Katie's or my confidence, or anyone else's within the club. That's a promise."

"Thank you. That's the thing, though. I'm not sure I'm with Ropes. I barely know him really. He's handsome, and sexy, and he makes me laugh, and feel beautiful, but…"

"But, what? He sounds great. He sounds like the guy I'd always pegged him as. I've always been so surprised that he didn't have women falling all over him. I thought maybe he was gay, but Clutch said he wasn't."

"Really? He's not a player? But he's so smooth and put together, I really would have thought he'd have a different girl every night."

"Not from what I've seen, so if you've caught his eye, I'm thinking you must be pretty special. You're obviously gorgeous, but the look in his eyes is more than attraction Devlin."

I swallowed nervously.

"Okay, twinkle toes. Let's get you off the table and into this wheelchair before that Valium kicks in."

As I navigated into my temporary mode of transportation, the room began to pulse along to the sound of my suddenly very present heartbeat.

"Oooh," I exclaimed and placed my hands on the arms of the chair to get my bearings.

"It's kicking in fast, huh?" Eldie asked as she wheeled

me back towards the exam room.

"I'd say."

I was a total lightweight when it came to anything stronger than a baby aspirin. The next few minutes were a bit hazy in my mind, but my memory involved something to do with penguins and a failed attempt at consuming a fruit cup.

"Devlin, sweetie, are you with me? This question is very important, so I need you to think long and hard before answering," Eldie said, as the effects of the meds she'd administered stepped into overdrive.

"Roger!" I said, with what was meant as a salute but ended up as a backhand to my own forehead.

"Okay, so the meds are doing their job," Katie said to Ropes as swirls of orange and blue light surrounded her like a halo of love and tranquility.

"Devlin, sweetie?" Eldie said.

"Uh huh."

"Here's the question... and remember it's important."

"I'm ready Doctor. Doctor... Dok-Tor, dahkter, you can say that a lot of different ways." The words trailed out of my mouth like cartoon balloon letters and then floated up to the ceiling.

"That's right, you sure can," Eldie said in a supportive tone. "Okay, here's the question. Are you ready?"

I tried to focus on what was sure to be a query of great medical importance.

"Which ice cream flavor do you like better? Chocolate or vanilla?"

I tried to fight through the ever-increasing Valium high and focus on the meaning of her question.

"Chocolate or vani—"

Pop.

The state of medicated bliss I was currently in was momentarily interrupted by the resetting of my broken toe. On a scale from one to ten, the pain was a seven, shoved up my ass sideways.

As it turns out, this seemingly sweet doctor, that had plied me with drugs and the sense that she took the Hippocratic oath very seriously, was nothing more than a barbaric war criminal who should probably have her baby taken away from her the minute it was born.

"Sorry, sweetie," I heard Dr. Evil say as I drifted into darkness.

Devlin

REENTERING CONSCIOUSNESS, I could hear Ropes and Eldie speaking in hushed tones. I couldn't make out much of what they were saying, but did manage to hear Ropes say, "She's really special," and, "Okay, but would that restrict her from going on a boat?"

This second piece of dialogue hastened my return from the spirit world.

"Why would I be on a boat?" I slurred.

"Good morning, sunshine," Ropes said sweetly as he stroked my hair.

"That Valium knocked you out. You must have really needed a nap," Eldie added.

"I'm a total wuss, I probably should have warned you."

"Probably for the best. Resetting that toe was no fun."

"Tell *me* about it," I scowled.

"Sorry about that," Eldie said. "The ice cream question is a dirty trick, but it always distracts the patient long enough for me to do what I need to do."

"How about waiting until I'm knocked out next time, huh?" I said, only half-jokingly.

"Whenever possible, we like patients to be alert when resetting small bone fractures. It sounds cruel, but it helps us to know when the bone is properly back in place if you're awake and your muscles aren't entirely relaxed. Trust me, it would have been a lot worse without the Valium or the local anesthetic."

"You gave me a local?"

"When I was examining you. Never felt it, did you?" Eldie smiled.

"You sneaky bitch," I hissed.

"That's Dr. Sneaky Bitch to you, Twinkle Toes," Eldie said, as she removed her medical gloves and disposed of them.

"Where's Katie?" I asked.

"Club get-together, so she headed out early. She said she's going to organize a girls' night out and you're required to go."

I chuckled. "Okay." I lifted my head from my pillow to make eye contact with Ropes. "Did I hear you say something about a boat?"

"You heard that, huh?" he asked sheepishly.

"Sort of. I was still waking up. What's going on?"

"It's the craziest thing," Ropes said, grinning like a little kid.

"Oh?"

"While you were in here with Eldie, I got an email from Olivia Stark and Ali Forrester," he said, still looking down at his phone.

"Are they a law firm or international jewel thieves?"

He raised an eyebrow. "They're romance writers. Really

good, very popular romance writers. Poised to be the next D.W. Foxblood."

"The author whose face you want to slice off and wear as your own?"

Ropes scowled, then whipped his head back and forth. "Where's Eldie? I need to know exactly when the effects of whatever the fuck she gave you are supposed to wear off."

"Oh, no sweetie. I'm sober as a judge, this is just me and my sick sense of humor."

"Once again, I must explain. I don't want to *be* D.W. Foxblood. I want to be *like* her."

I shrugged. "Tomato... Face Off, either way."

Ropes continued, "Anyway. Every year, Olivia and Ali host an event called the Books and Booze Cruise. It's a three-day weekend at sea where authors and readers mingle. The events are always legendary, and a ton of great authors attend. This year D.W. Foxblood will be attending."

"Sounds like fun. Was the email about tickets still being available or something?"

"More like or something, it's always sold-out." Ropes's expression changed from delight to panic.

"What's wrong?"

"They've invited me to be a signing author on this year's cruise."

"What? You're kidding me? That's great news... isn't it?" I wasn't sure, by the look on Ropes's face if this was in fact good news.

"I don't know what to tell them."

"Tell them yes, dummy!" I yelled.

"But they're like big-time, legit authors and I'm an absolute zero."

I was a little shocked to hear Ropes, who'd always carried himself as the picture of confidence, say this. I didn't get the impression that this was false modesty in any form either. He truly felt like he was somehow "less than" these other authors.

"Look," I said sternly. "I've never read a romance book in my life. Hell, I'm not sure I've finished any book since school, so I don't know who any of these people are, but I know for a fact, they all started somewhere... at the start."

"Yeah, but they're all established now, as are most of the other authors on the cruise."

"But not all of them, right?" I asked. "They invite new authors as well?"

"That's why they've reached out to me. Apparently, Olivia Stark read my last MC book and passed it on to Ali Forrester. They both loved it and have asked if I would attend this year's event."

"That's amazing. See. They're inviting you because they like you!"

"But I've only released three books. How the heck did they even hear about me?"

"Sweetie," I said softly. "This is how the world works y'know. The important thing is that they reached out and that you're going to say yes."

"But Eldie says you're gonna need to wear a boot for four weeks and the cruise is in two," he said.

"Who said I'm going with you?"

"There's no way in hell I'm going without you."

Well, that was seriously sweet. "Well, if you can put up with gimpy me, I'll do my best to keep up."

He grinned, leaning down to kiss me. "You're not gimpy, you're just a leg down at the moment. Kind of like a pirate."

"Arrrrrg," I exclaimed, interrupting our kiss. "Where's the cruise going?"

"I'm not sure, to be honest." He waggled his eyebrows at me. "But I know it's somewhere you'll be required to wear a bikini."

I rolled my eyes. "I'll try to find something that'll match my super-sexy boot."

He leaned down and grinned before kissing me gently. "I like that idea."

"I bet you do."

Once I was cleared to head home, Ropes gently loaded me in Ben and we headed to my place where he spent the next few hours catering to my every need.

Falling in love with this man might just be the best decision I'd ever made.

* * *

Ropes

"What is this?" Minus yelled as he burst through my door.

"What the hell?" I protested, bolting up from my bed.

Minus scowled. "I asked you a question," he said, holding the copy of my book that I'd given him high above his head. "What the fuck is this?"

"Looks like a book," I replied wiping the sleep from my eyes.

"Very funny. Ropes, how long have we known each other?" Minus asked but cut me off before I could answer. "A long fuckin' time, that's how long. So, how come in all that time you never told me that you could write like this?"

"What? Are you serious?"

"When you first told me about writing romance, I honestly thought you and the club were fucking with me, but then I read your book and I could tell that you'd actually written this. I could hear your voice within the characters. I may not be the demographic, but I thought this was really good."

"I don't know what to say, I'm a little shocked honestly."

"If you say there's money to be made for the club, then I'll sign off on giving you the time and resources needed to take this venture to the next level," Minus said, extending his hand.

"That's great, but I can take care of my own expenses."

"You sure?" Minus asked.

"I may have left my family's money behind, but I kept every grain of knowledge I learned from them about business. My investments are solid, have no debt, and I'm flush for cash. You allowing me the time to write and travel will be plenty. The timing couldn't be better, too."

"Why's that?"

"I've been invited to my first big signing event."

"Time to get out there and sink or swim huh?"

"You have no idea how right you are."

* * *

"This is fucking worse than I fucking ever could have fucking imagined!" The veins in Wolf's neck bulged and spit flew from his mouth as he bellowed. Minus, in stark contrast, remained perfectly calm seated at his desk, hands neatly folded.

"Did you grow up on a fuck farm or do you buy them wholesale?" I asked glibly.

"Your mom gives them to me, and here's one just for you. Fuck you, Ropes," he snapped.

The fact that Wolf had brought my mother into this, even if it was in the most juvenile of ways, made me want to whale on him until the shit he was full of came out his ears. Did Wolf forget that my mother was dead before taking such a cheap shot, or worse, did he know full well? Either way, I had to let it slide. Wolf held rank over me, and I couldn't do shit about it.

"You seem to have reservations about this plan," Minus said, coolly.

"Reser-fucking-vations? No, I don't have reservations, Minus. I think this whole thing is the stupidest fucking idea I've ever heard in my entire fucking life."

"There's that word again. I think I'm getting you a thesaurus for Christmas this year."

Wolf took an ill-intentioned step toward me and Minus immediately rose to his feet.

"Stow that shit right now," he growled. "You've been at each other like a hen and a duck since Cutter died and I'm sick of hearing it. So, sit the fuck down and we can talk about this like men, or you can get the fuck outta my office and I'll *tell* you both what your next fuckin' job is. Got it?"

Wolf and I gave each other a reluctant nod and sat down.

"First of all, Ropes, show your Captain some respect and give your mouth a rest." I nodded and Minus turned his attention to Wolf. "I asked everyone to come up with legal ways for the club to earn. I asked every member to be crea-

113

tive, and Ropes did what his President asked. As his Road Captain, you should be proud of him."

"It ain't just that," Wolf snapped.

"Then what's the problem?" Minus returned to his seat.

"The whole fuckin' going straight thing. I think it's bullshit."

"You've made that crystal clear on multiple occasions, Wolf, and every time I've reminded you that this is the way Cutter wanted it, and that you're free to patch out at any time."

"Cutter is dead, and I've been in this club since you were trading boogers in the sandbox." Wolf leaned in. "I'm not fucking going anywhere, and if you're feeling strong enough to come at me with the brand, take your best shot."

"Be very careful brother. As long as you wear that patch, you'll abide by the code. Like it or not, Cutter gave me Red Dog's staff. He gave me the burden of leading this club and he gave me a plan, a plan that I intend to follow. Not just because I want to honor his memory, but because I believe it means the survival of this club."

"What's the point of being outlaw bikers if we're not outlaws anymore?"

"Let me ask you a question. Did you start riding bikes in order to become a criminal?"

"No, both things just sort of happened I guess," Wolf replied.

"So, the fact that you love to ride has nothing to do with how you make a living out on the streets?"

"I don't think so."

"Then what does it matter how you earn, or whether or not it's legal or illegal? I know what you're afraid of, Wolf."

"I ain't fuckin' afraid of anything."

"Yes, you are, and it's the same thing that every member of this club is afraid of. It's also the very thing I'm trying to steer us away from."

"What?"

"Obsolescence."

"You keep saying shit like that and I still don't know

what you mean."

"What made Cutter a great president?" Minus asked.

"I dunno, he was tough I guess," Wolf replied.

"Sure, he was, but do you really think that's what made him a great father to the club? Give it some thought, you knew the man for over twenty-five years."

Wolf paused for a moment before replying, "He was a smart motherfucker."

"Yes, he was. He also knew how and when to change with the times. When he started the Burning Saints, he had no juice on the streets and no money, so he did what he had to do to get things going. As soon as the club was established and stable, he moved away from street hustles and established one of the biggest protection services this country has never heard of. He managed to do all of this without him or any of his officers ever seeing the inside of a Federal prison cell."

"So, what's your point?"

"My point is, Cutter could no longer envision that chapter of the club continuing. He knew, as well as I do, that times have changed in ways we could have never imagined. The days of the outlaw biker aren't numbered Wolf, they're finished, and if we want to keep riding together as a family, we have to adapt."

"Jesus, Minus. You make it all sound so easy. We have blood on our hands, man. That shit don't just wash off because you've decided to move from chop shops to flower shops. You've dug holes and you've helped fill some, we all have. You think the Feds won't care about that shit just because Cutter felt guilty at the end?"

"You don't know what you're talking about," Minus snapped.

"The fuck I don't. I've seen it time and again. This shit happens to a lot of the old-timers when they come to the end of the road, or they've been locked up long enough, they get soft, or they get Jesus."

"Cutter never lost his shit, or his edge and you know it. It's why no one challenged him when he named me as his successor."

Wolf glanced down.

"What? You think I didn't know there's been grumbling within the ranks since day fucking one? Cutter knew it was gonna happen and I did too, but no one challenged Cutter then because they knew better, and no one's challenged me openly since he died because, despite your bitching, not one of you has starved to death."

"We ain't exactly thriving, though are we?" Wolf growled.

"What do you think I'm trying to do here, Wolf? I'm trying to find new ways for the club to thrive."

"By selling Ropes's Penthouse Forum letters?"

"Fuck, you're old," I said, unable to stop myself.

"What the fuck did I tell you, Ropes?"

"I'm sorry, Minus, but he's sitting here calling my writing cheap 80's porn," I protested.

"And you're gonna sit there and shut the hell up while he does if that's what I tell you to do." He turned to Wolf. "And you're gonna follow orders whether you like it or not. I didn't bring you in here to ask your permission to move forward with Ropes's plan, but you were his Road Captain, so I wanted to give you a head's up."

"What the fuck do you mean I was his Road Captain?" Wolf rose to his feet. "If you think you're taking my Captain patch—"

"Settle down, Wolf, I'm not taking anything from anyone," Minus said as he rose. "Cutter never saw the need for the club to have a treasurer and handled all the bookkeeping himself. In fact, there were only two people he ever sought advice from regarding financial matters. Duke, my mentor in Savannah, and you, Ropes."

"What?" I asked, completely shocked by this bit of information.

"When you first came to the Club and told Cutter about your background he had a feeling that you'd be a good resource, and he was right."

"What are you talking about? Cutter and I never discussed the club's finances. Not even once."

"Sure, you did. You just didn't know it." Minus smiled. "Cutter said he was constantly picking your brain about the stock market."

"He'd read some article in the Financial Times or the Journal and ask my opinion about it, sure, but nothing more."

"Nothing more than idle business chit-chat to you maybe, but he'd listen to you and make investments with the club's money. Investments that are starting to see some major returns."

"Are you serious?"

"Yes, and I'm now at the point where I need someone to help manage our money."

"I thought Cricket's been handling all that," I replied.

"She has, but I need her focused in other areas now. It's time the club had an official Treasurer and I want that person to be you, Ropes."

I didn't know who was more stunned, me or Wolf.

"Congratulations, Ropes. You deserve this," Minus said, shaking my hand. "Wolf, Ropes is no longer in your crew, he's your fellow officer. I expect you two to work together... without issue."

"I'm cool," I said, extending a hand to Wolf, who simply looked at it momentarily before shaking it.

"Whatever. I still think this is all fucking weird."

"Look, I don't expect Ropes to get rich off this book thing, but he's agreed to cut the club in on the profits in return for dedicated time to write. He's honored the code by not withholding and by coming to me with this, so we're gonna do right by him.

"I appreciate it, Minus."

"You've earned it. The financial advice you gave Cutter is making money for us, and with you officially patched as Treasurer, I have a feeling there's gonna be a lot more where that came from. So long as we're seeing profit, we're gonna support you and see where this all goes."

Wolf nodded and Minus dismissed him, leaving the two of us alone.

"I honestly don't know what to say."

"I meant what I said about you deserving a seat at the table. You've got skills and you've been a loyal soldier since day one. We came up in this club together, and you and your brother should have been officers by now. I'm gonna make that right because it's the right thing to do, and the right move for the club."

Minus and I embraced, and I thanked him again.

"Keep this info close to the kutte for now, and we'll have an official blow out when you get back from the high seas."

FOURTEEN

BURNING SAINTS

Devlin

ROPES HAULED OUR bags into an Uber while I climbed into the back. It took me a little more time to manage with my boot, and I was grateful I didn't have to deal with luggage as well. Ropes assured me that I still looked great despite my new accessory, but I was counting down the days until I didn't have to wear this stupid thing anymore.

Our flight from Portland to Ft. Lauderdale had been uneventful and the airline staff had been amazing, going above and beyond in helping me get settled. Thankfully, Ropes had splurged for first-class, and I knew the second we sat down and were offered a glass of champagne, I was going to love everything about this trip.

Arriving at the port, Ropes helped me out of the car, then

organized for our bags to be loaded onto carts and taken directly to our room. I kept my backpack with ID and essentials, and he did the same, then we headed to the ship boarding.

An attendant ushered us to a line away from the masses and we went through security and then followed where directed, into what we'd come to find out was the VIP line. We were there not because of our importance, but because of my air cast.

"Your fancy footwear's makin' this easier," Ropes said with a grin.

"Glad my clumsiness could be of assistance," I retorted, and he kissed me gently.

"Really glad you're with me, baby."

"Me too."

I leaned against him and heard him hiss out, "Holy shit, it's D.W. Foxblood."

I glanced up at him, then followed his line of sight to see a petite, casually-dressed red-haired woman walking by us. She was beautiful and was accompanied by an equally attractive man that I assumed was her husband. What I found most interesting, was that I recognized the man.

"I know him from somewhere." I whispered as the couple neared us.

"Who?" Ropes asked, distractedly.

"The guy she's with. I can't put my finger on it, but I know him."

"Clay?" D.W. asked as she approached.

Ropes, clearly startled, managed to squeak out, "Hey," in return.

"I'm D.W., it's so nice to meet you," she said warmly, throwing her arms around a clearly stunned Ropes.

"I'm sorry, you'll have to forgive me," Ropes sputtered. "Of course, I know who you are, I'm just completely shocked that you know who I am."

"I told Ali and Olivia that I'm a big fan of your work and I meant it," she replied.

"I—" was all Ropes could manage.

D.W. Foxblood was currently one of the hottest properties in the literary world. Her wildly successful first book, Forbidden Pleasures had thrust her into the spotlight and had even spawned a series of movies starring singer-turned-actress Melody Morgan.

She smiled. "They didn't tell you that you're the reason that I agreed to come on the cruise?"

When D.W. said she loved his books, Ropes looked like someone had just told him he was about to have twins. Now he looked like he was also going to carry and deliver them.

He managed to spit out, "No, they did not."

"Not only do I enjoy your stories, but there's a level of authenticity in your writing that really grabs me. It's what first got me hooked. I sent you an email once, but I never heard back."

"I deleted that when I saw it," Ropes said, turning pale. "I thought it was spam. I never, in a million years would have thought that'd actually come from one of your people."

"My people?" D.W. looked at her companion and they burst out laughing, before she cut herself off with a gasp. "I'm sorry, how rude of me. This is my husband, Mack," she said, placing a hand on his shoulder.

The moment she said his name I realized exactly where I knew him from but said nothing.

"And this is my..." Ropes paused and looked at me before continuing, "girlfriend, Devlin."

I shook D.W.'s hand first and then Mack's, who's eyes locked on mine.

"Devlin, right?" he said, smiling wide.

"You know each other?" D.W. asked.

"You work at Fat Donny's place on Hawthorne, right?" Mack asked.

"Sometimes," I replied.

"I came in with a guy named Finch a few months ago."

"I remember. He'd just patched in. I did his first club tattoo. Dogs of Fire, right?"

"You're in the Dogs?" Ropes asked, clearly taken aback. "I knew you rode but—"

"And you ride with the Burning Saints," Mack said discretely.

Ropes head snapped to D.W.

"I told you I'm a big fan, *Ropes*," she said with a wink and a smile.

"Holy shit, I had no idea," he stammered. "What are the fucking odds?"

"I always say there are only two dozen people in all of Portland, so be nice because you're gonna run into every one of them eventually."

"I'm happy to meet both of you. I'm still kind of in shock about all of this to be honest with you."

"When I read your books, I knew I had to meet you, so when you didn't reply to my email I had a guy in the club do some digging on you. That's when we found out who you are and who you ride with. I knew from your writing that you had to be an actual club member, or at least be tight with one."

"What did you mean when you said I was the reason you'd accepted Olivia and Ali's invitation?"

"It's not like it took much convincing," D.W. smiled. "They've been inviting me for years, but my schedule's been a little crazy, so it just hasn't worked out. We've still kept in touch and we trade books all the time, that's how I got turned on to the Clay Morningwood books. I don't have as much time for reading as I'd like and am always excited when a book really grabs me."

"Thank you, so much. I can't tell you how much that means to me, coming from you." Ropes laughed. "I just still can't believe that D.W. Foxblood was stalking me."

"Please, call me Darien," she replied with a curtsy.

"Ropes," he replied. "But, apparently you knew that."

"You have a guy in your club that runs background checks?" I asked.

"Booker comes in handy," Mack said. "I'm not sure he's as good as Kitty..." he said raising an eyebrow, referring to the ex-Dog, hacker, and current Burning Saints' houseguest.

"Word travels fast," Ropes replied.

"Only two dozen people," Darien reiterated with a smile.

The security line moved on and we eventually made our way on board the massive vessel. Once we were checked in, we made plans to meet up with Darien and Mack later for drinks and said goodbye for now.

Ropes was wired as we headed to our room. I could tell he was trying to keep himself in check, but I honestly expected him to start waving his hands in front of his face and fangirling in front of Darien. She and Mack were really cool, so I was looking forward to getting to know them over the next few days.

We found our room and Ropes unlocked the door and pushed it open, standing back so I could precede him inside. I walked into a surprisingly large room, complete with queen-sized bed, small sofa, desk and chair, and a balcony. We'd found one of our bags sitting in the hallway, so he lugged that in as well.

"This is so nice," I said, as he followed me in. I stood at the slider and stared outside. The sun was glistening off the water and I wished I could swim.

"Yeah, it looks great," he agreed, hauling the suitcase onto the bed.

I grinned and faced him, dropping my backpack on top of the suitcase. "If you wouldn't mind moving that stuff, I'd like a quickie before we have to do that muster drill thingy."

I didn't have to ask twice as he dumped everything on the floor before lifting me and dropping me gently onto the bed. I laughed as he lifted my shirt and kissed my belly. "I like this side of you, honey," I said, as he kissed his way up my body.

He knelt between my legs and pushed my skirt up. "And I like this side of *you*. Easy access." He tugged on my panties. "Lift."

I lifted my hips and he pulled them down my legs, maneuvering them over my boot, then dropping them on the floor before burying his face in my pussy.

I wrapped my good leg over his shoulder and arched up, weaving my hands in his hair. As he sucked my clit, he slid one finger, then two inside of me, pumping harder and harder until I exploded around him. He didn't give me much time to relish in my orgasm, standing to remove his clothes, then hovering over me again.

Kissing me, he slid into me and I gripped his ass, begging him to go deeper. He slipped his hand under my T-shirt and tugged a bra cup down, fingering my nipple into a tight bead as he rocked into me.

"Ropes," I hissed.

"What, baby?" he asked, burying himself deeper.

"That."

He grinned, rocking again, before slamming into me over and over again. I cried out his name, dragging my nails down his back as an orgasm washed over me and he continued to move until I felt his cock pulse inside of me. I kissed him again, smiling against his lips. "You are so very, very good at that."

He chuckled. "Glad you appreciate my efforts."

He slid out of me and walked behind the closet, returning with a warm washcloth, placing it between my legs. "Feel good?"

"It feels amazing," I said. "Thank you."

He headed back into the bathroom while I stayed on the bed for a few minutes, my foot suddenly throbbing. "Honey."

"Yeah," he called back.

"Can you please find me a painkiller?"

He walked into view in all his naked glory with a frown and started rummaging in my backpack. "How bad's the pain?"

"A bit like an icepick being shoved into the bone, but otherwise, not so bad."

He found my prescription and popped open the bottle, pouring one into his palm. He helped me sit up and handed me the pill, then grabbed some water so I could take it. "We might have overdone it, huh?" he asked, sitting beside me.

"Bite your tongue," I admonished. "I love everything we did just then. I wouldn't change a thing."

He grinned. "You're one tough bitch, baby."

"Hey, I'm not a bitch," I joked. "Well, unless I'm your biker bitch, of course."

"You're my *perfect* biker bitch," he assured me, kissing me gently. "Come on, you sit here while I unpack." He lifted me onto the little sofa, then hauled the bag on the bed again.

* * *

Ropes

The white noise of Devlin's hairdryer and the low, steady hum of the ship's engines were acting as a powerful sleep agent. The fact that we'd already fucked, had a hot shower, then fucked again before we'd even left port didn't help either. I was blissfully drained and losing the battle to keep my eyelids open as I lie on our stateroom bed.

"Good afternoon ladies and gentlemen, this is your captain speaking, welcoming you aboard the Calliope," a smooth, heavily accented voice came across the ship's P.A. system, and Devlin killed the hair dryer. *"As you may have noticed, the ship's engines have started, which means we will be departing shortly. At this time, I would like to inform you of a mandatory muster station drill that will be taking place in just ten minutes. Please check the plaque located on the rear of your cabin door for your assigned muster station."*

The captain finished his muster instructions, and the mere thought of schlepping through the ship with a lifejacket on only made me feel even more tired.

"You're gonna have to go on without me," I groaned. "You can... muster for the both of us."

"I don't think that's how this works," Devlin replied as she returned to her hair.

"I can barely move."

"You were moving just fine a few minutes ago buddy."

"That's the problem. You broke me, now I can't move, and it's all your fault."

"You're gonna have to do a lot more than move. We have the registration cocktail party at four o'clock, and

Clay's gonna need to have his game face on."

"Son of a motherless goat," I exclaimed, sitting up quickly.

Devlin shot back, startled. "What?"

"I'm gonna have to talk to readers."

Devlin smiled. "Yeah, that's kind of the point of this whole thing isn't it?"

"I guess I was so nervous about meeting the other authors, especially D.W., that I must have put the readers out of my mind. Now that I've met her and the adrenaline is wearing off, I'm realizing I, or rather Clay, has to talk to readers."

"What's the problem? You're a well-spoken, friendly guy."

"Ropes is, sure. But what about Clay?"

"What do you mean?" Devlin truly looked puzzled.

I started grabbing for random items of clothing from my suitcase, barely paying any mind to what I was doing.

"I spent the first part of my life as Spencer and I guess I never really liked who that guy was entirely. Then I became Ropes, but that felt more like my identity as a biker, a club member."

"And Clay?"

"Writing as Clay Morningwood was never supposed to be anything serious. I started writing novels as a challenge to myself. I wanted to know if I had the ability to write about club life and make it appealing to the masses. Once I really started digging in, I discovered the MC romance genre, and the community of independent authors within it, and before I knew it, Clay was off and running."

Devlin stopped my frantic unpacking and stroked my cheek. "This means a lot to you now doesn't it?"

"It does, and that's why I'm afraid of screwing it up."

"How would you do that exactly?"

"What if I don't know how to *be* Clay?" I asked.

"What do you mean?"

"I know how to write as Clay, but I've never had to be Clay in person. I'm not sure I really know who he is in public."

"Isn't he just you?"

"I guess, in a way, sure. But he's also another person entirely. Sort of like a superhero suit that I'm called to step into when needed."

"I would think, as an extrovert, you'd have no problem talking to strangers."

"That's the thing. Since I'm outgoing and talkative, people always assume I'm an extrovert."

"You're not?"

"I don't think so. By classic definition, an extrovert is someone who gets charged up when around other people, whereas I prefer to be alone most of the time."

"I wouldn't have guessed that."

"That's because I've barely been alone since our first date."

"That wasn't a date." Devlin smiled, and I kissed her.

"Whatever it was, I haven't wanted to be away from you since, which makes it a little hard to write if I'm being honest."

"I thought I was your muse."

"You are, and you inspire new ideas every day, but at some point, I'm gonna need to lock myself away for a little while and finish this book."

"Oh, I'm sorry, have I been a distraction?" Devlin asked as she pulled her shirt up over her perfect tits.

"I'd like to say that's not very helpful, but suddenly I am feeling a lot better."

Devlin leaned in for a kiss this time. "You're going to be great. Just be yourself, whoever that is, and I know everyone will love you."

"As long as you like me, I'll be just fine."

"Are you kidding? I'm Clay Morningwood's number one fan."

"I think you might be the sole member of my fan club."

"Not according to Darien and all your other author friends."

"First of all, they are not my friends. I'd be lucky to call them professional acquaintances. Secondly, I think they're being polite to a new author."

"I may not be an expert on the topic of romance writing, but I'm pretty good at identifying bullshitters, and Darien loved your writing."

"Maybe so, but I still feel like a complete imposter here. Besides D.W., Olivia, and Ali, there are a ton of other big authors that have been in the game for a long time. Who the hell even knows I exist? I probably have no reason to be scared to talk to the readers, since my table will be empty tomorrow anyway."

"Wow!" Devlin exclaimed. "Are you getting dizzy from all that spiraling?"

"See, this is the shit I'm talking about. The side of me that no one ever sees."

"It's totally refreshing, to be honest with you."

"What?"

"And highly entertaining." Devlin smiled wide.

"I'm so glad my existential melt down is a source of your amusement."

"Can you blame me? It's a little hard being around Mr. Perfect all the time?"

"Mr. Perfect? Are you shitting me?" I spat out in utter shock.

"You're always so put together and quick with your words. You seem to float through a room with a confidence I've never seen before. I get the sense that you already know what's going to happen in advance. Like, not only can you read the room, but that you're already thinking three steps ahead of everyone else."

It was hard to reconcile Devlin's perception of me with what I was feeling, but I knew she was being honest. "This is why you're my muse. You see things within me that I don't. You pull the best parts out of me and drag them into the light."

"If you say I make you want to be a better man, I swear I'll jump overboard before we even leave port."

As if on cue, the muster drill alarm sounded off, and we joined our fellow passengers on deck, at our assigned station.

FIFTEEN

BURNING SAINTS

Devlin

WE STOOD BY one of the ship's many outdoor bars for the duration of the muster drill, which mostly consisted of the captain reading from a script about staying calm should we hit an iceberg or whatever. To be honest, I wasn't paying very close attention. What I was focused on, was the gaggle of women that were staring at Ropes as if he were a piece of meat on a hook. Of course, he seemed totally oblivious which made me wonder if I was just being jealous.

Wait a minute. Was I jealous? I'm not certain I'd know for sure because, to my knowledge, it's never been an emotion I'd had to wrestle with. Perhaps I'd just never cared enough about a person to get jealous.

"Anything you'd like to share with the rest of the class?" Ropes asked with a smile.

"Sorry, just lost in thought I guess."

"You're not thinking of hopping onto one of those lifeboats and leaving me here without you, are you?"

"Nope, just hope I don't have to cut a bitch while out at sea."

"Thinking of taking up piracy as a profession?"

"No, more like bodyguard to the stars. I think Clay Morningwood might have more fans than you think."

Ropes scanned the area and I noticed eyes turning away from him as he did. His presence was known, and I was pretty sure I wasn't crazy.

"I think you'll be much busier as a full-time tattoo artist," he murmured.

The captain announced the end of the drill, and Ropes and I made our way back to the room to stow our life vests before the scheduled meet and greet cocktail party.

"Speaking of which, your club doesn't appear to wear much ink," I said as we walked.

"Apart from my brother and a couple other guys that's mostly true."

"Why's that?"

"Mostly because our guys don't tend to spend much time in prison. Cutter was a smart president and worked hard to keep us a step ahead of the cops. Apart from some stints in county and few state bids, most of our members nationwide have relatively clean records."

"That's surprising."

"Cutter was a great president and a great man."

"It sounds like you miss him."

"Every day."

I freshened up and we made our way to the Skylight Lounge, where the event's registration table was set up.

The moment we walked into the lounge we were greeted by two beautiful women standing underneath a giant Books and Booze Cruise banner. One woman was tall with purple hair, and the other was a brunette and held a clipboard in one hand and a walkie talkie in the other.

"Clay!" the brunette squealed in delight as soon as she spotted him, and the two ran toward us.

"I'm going to have to get used to calling you Clay," I whispered just before being showered in hugs by our hosts.

"We're so glad you could make it," the brunette welcomed us warmly.

"Thank you so much for inviting me. I'm still not sure what I'm doing here, but I'm excited," Ropes said, sounding uncharacteristically nervous, before introducing me. "I'm sorry, this is Devlin, my..."

"Clay's personal security detail," I said, playfully poking Ropes in the ribs.

"I'm Ali and this is Olivia," the brunette said, motioning to the other woman, who had, until then, been silent.

"A word of warning," Ali leaned in to whisper. "Olivia said if anyone hands you a glass of something blue, don't drink it," she warned, stabilizing herself on the registration table.

"Not good, huh?" I asked.

"No, reeeeeeeally good," she said, grinning from ear to ear.

"It's called a Captain Blue Breeze, and she's had six so far," Ali said in a mock den mother voice.

"That you know of," Olivia sassed back.

Clearly the booze part of the cruise was under way and these women were not fooling around.

"Sounds like we've got some catching up to do, baby," Ropes said.

Every time he called me baby goosebumps ran up the back of my neck. No one had ever called me baby before, and I'm quite sure if they had, I'd have squashed that shit immediately. Normally, I hated gushy sentimentality and things like pet names, but for some reason, when it came from Ropes's lips, it felt genuine and truly romantic.

"I'll race you to the bar, sailor," I joked.

"Here are your registration packets and name badges," Ali said. "The bar is open and on us tonight, so don't use your drink cards. The cocktail party is all about meeting your fellow authors and drinking until you've forgotten you've met them."

We grabbed our bags, made our way through the crowd, found a spot at an empty table in the corner, and Ropes ordered us a couple of Bahama Mamas.

"This is delicious," I said, taking a sip of the fruity concoction. "Plus, rum makes me frisky," I said, with a wink.

Just then, a handsome young man wearing a shiny silver coat, a priest's collar, and a camouflage fanny pack hopped onto the lounge's stage with a microphone.

"How is everyone feeling tonight, cruisers?" he shouted to a round of tepid cheers. "Apparently, we have a lot of first timers on board with us this year. Let's try that again? How we feelin' Books and Booze cruisers?"

This time the room erupted, and the shiny man smiled wide. "That's more like it. My name is Father Finn Edward Peck and I'll be your emcee on the high seas. We're gonna kick things off tonight with a little something we like to call 'the confessional.'"

The DJ took his cue and dance music pumped throughout the lounge's sound system.

"Who's going to be first to step into my confessional?" Father Finn asked, motioning to an empty chair sitting on the stage, as a spotlight began scanning the room. "Who's got sins to confess? Come on now, don't be shy."

I don't know what came over me, maybe the rum was kicking in, but in a moment of pure spontaneity, I grabbed Ropes's wrist, and thrust his hand high in the air.

"What the hell are you doing?" he protested as I attempted, unsuccessfully to keep him from lowering his hand. Our playful struggle caught the attention of Father Finn.

"We have our first confessor!" he shouted gleefully.

"What? No, no, no," Ropes said waving his hands, as Father Finn motioned him to join him on stage.

"Come on, it'll only hurt a little, I promise."

The room erupted into applause and Ropes sheepishly rose to his feet.

"You are going to pay for this," he said through a smile, and made his way to the stage.

"Come on up, sinner, it's time to confess. What's your name, cruiser?" Father Finn asked, shoving the microphone in Ropes's face.

"Ro... Clay, Clay Morningwood," he replied, quickly correcting himself.

"Are you a reader or an author?"

"I'm an author, and this is my first cruise."

"We've got ourselves a virgin," he shouted to more applause. "Take a seat, Clay Morningwood and prepare to cleanse your soul."

Ropes did as he was asked, and Father Finn continued, "The object of this game is to be as honest as possible. Every time we think you're not being completely truthful, we're all going to take a drink," he said, motioning to the room. "Got it?"

Ropes nodded and swallowed hard.

"Okay, time to confess your sins. First question, how old were you when you lost your virginity?" The room let out a series of whoops and hollers.

"Wow, jumping right in," Ropes said, clearing his throat. "I guess I got started a little early. I was fourteen years old."

"What do we think cruisers? Was that a true confession?"

The crowd cheered in approval and Father Finn continued, "Moving on then. When is the last time you woke up in a stranger's bed after a night of partying?"

"Never," he responded immediately.

"What say all of you?"

"Bullshit!" a woman's voice called out from the back of the room.

"You heard the lady, drink up," Father Finn said, and glasses lifted all around.

"What?" Ropes protested with a smile. "That was the truth."

"Sorry, Clay, the congregation simply does not believe you. Oh, I forgot to mention one thing, every time they don't believe you, they take a sip, but you have to do two shots," he said, as Ali walked onto the stage with a tray lined with shot glasses.

Ropes laughed and, like a good sport, downed two shots.

"Okay, let's move on to question number three. Have you ever committed a crime?"

Ropes shifted in his seat. "Um… nothing serious," he said, and immediately the entire room collectively took a drink.

"I think it's pretty clear what you need to do," Finn said, and Ropes emptied two more shot glasses.

"Okay, Clay. Here's your final question. Have you ever been in love?"

A hush fell across the room and Ropes paused for a moment before turning his gaze to me. He leaned into the microphone and delivered a decisive, "Yes."

Every glass in the lounge remained in place as did Ropes's stare.

"Your sins have been absolved," Father Finn shouted. Music began pumping while lights strobed and flashed. Two shirtless male book cover models, wearing angels' wings, presented Clay with a cardboard treasure chest, covered in gold glitter. The chest was filled with sex toys of various shapes, sizes and applications. "Time for you to go to heaven," he said, handing Clay his eternal reward, tilting the microphone toward his mouth.

"Umm… Amen?" Clay said softly.

"Amen indeed!" Finn exclaimed to a large round of applause from the crowd. This cruise was shaping up to be very interesting.

Ropes

I SCANNED THE dining room for a friendly face and it didn't take long before I found one.

"Clay, over here!" Olivia smiled and waved me over to her table. I arrived to find her sitting with a large group of what appeared to be readers.

"It's wonderful to see you tonight, Mrs. Stark, you look lovely."

"Thank you so much, you clean up pretty nicely yourself sir," Olivia said.

"Where's Ali?" I asked, curious to see the dynamic duo apart.

"We try to make it a point to spread the authors out as much as possible during the dinners. It gives the readers a chance to get to know as many writers as possible. Tonight, I get to sit with these amazing people," she said with a natural warmth.

"Hi, I'm Clay," I said, cheerily to the table, who all responded back in kind, except one woman, who simply sat there with a scowl on her face. I took a stab at catching the name on her laminate, but it had flipped around. However, I did spot that she was wearing an author's lanyard around her neck.

I've been in enough online writer's groups to know that most are introverts, who, on any given day, would likely prefer to be by themselves or with a trusted friend. Mixing and mingling with strangers, nice as they may be, is not always easy for people who sit alone in silence, writing for hours on end. I have endless amounts of grace for my fellow writers when it comes to this, and figured she was simply a little more reserved.

"Hey there." I turned my full attention to the author. "I don't think we've met, I'm Clay Morningwood," I said, extending a hand, which she eyeballed as if I were offering her a used tissue.

"Yeah, I saw you last night," she said, in a dismissive tone that made me feel about three inches tall.

Not wanting to leave that awkwardness floating over the table, I tried once again to break the ice. "Yeah, that was pretty crazy. Finn seems like a fun guy to hang with, right?"

"Sure."

Maybe I was imagining things, but this woman did not appear to be a fan of yours truly.

"I'm sorry, your tag is flipped around, what's your name?" I asked, and her vibe changed from merely dismissive to straight up ice queen.

"I'm Val Weston," she replied, but may as well have screamed, *"Don't you know who I am?"* but I didn't have a fucking clue, and judging by the attitude she was giving off, didn't have much of a desire to find out.

"Clay writes MC books as well," Olivia said to Val.

"I've never heard of you," she said through pursed lips.

Olivia wore an expression like that of a hostage victim trying not to tip the bad guys off while signaling the police.

"I've read your books and I love them," the woman seated next to Val said.

Val's head snapped to her.

"Really, you do?" I asked, genuinely shocked.

The woman nodded.

"I've still never heard of you," Val said, increasing the disdain in her voice.

"I'm pretty new at all of this. I've only released a handful of books so far," I said, keeping my tone sweet.

Olivia tried, once again to ease the tension, "Val's new book just made the bestseller's list today, right Val?"

"Yesterday," she said without making eye contact with Olivia.

"Congratulations," I said, smiling, and with that, Val Weston turned and began talking quietly with the woman next to her as if I wasn't even standing there.

"Where's your gorgeous lady? She's not seasick, is she?" Olivia asked, thankfully pulling me away from award-winning twat-pocket, Val Weston.

I grinned. "No, she's great. Just running a little behind due to her boot. She didn't want to miss out on a good spot, so she sent me ahead."

"Poor thing, what happened?"

"Let's just say Devlin and her bedroom dresser should no longer be dance partners," I replied.

Val leaned over and whispered something in her neighbor's ear, before she returned to giving me the stink eye. I had no idea what I'd done to offend this woman, and perhaps I was just being paranoid, but she seemed to take issue with my very presence.

"Speak of the angel," Olivia said, and I turned to see Devlin enter the dining room. Olivia stood and waved Devlin toward us, and I excused myself to meet her.

"You look amazing," I said as I helped her down the steps into the lower level of the dining room.

"I wish I didn't have to wear this stupid boot."

"Imagine you're Cinderella and it's your glass slipper."

"The only princess that was ever worth more than two shits was Princess Leia, and that was only because she fought to the rank of General."

I stopped her mid-stride and pulled her in for a kiss. I didn't give a shit that we were in the middle of the dining room and all eyes were upon us. As a matter of fact, I was more than fine with everyone on the boat knowing full-well that I was completely into this woman.

"I didn't know Star Wars talk got you all hot and bothered." Devlin smiled.

"*You* get me all hot and bothered."

"Good answer," she replied.

"I'm curious though. You showed zero love to the pinball nerds back at the bar and yet seem to know a lot about Star Wars, Monty Python, and comic books. What's up with that? Are you a closeted nerd?"

"I'm not a nerd, I'm just pop culture aware," Devlin protested.

"Whatever, Poindexter."

I guided us back to Olivia's table where Val Weston's blank expression had now graduated into a full on scowl.

"Hi sweetie, how are you? You look beautiful," Olivia said, rising to hug Devlin.

"Thank you so much," she replied. "You and Ali have been so sweet, I don't know how to thank you both. Is she around?"

"She's probably somewhere making a list or checking items off a list," she said with a chuckle. "All you have to do is relax, have fun, and do your best to max out your drink package limit every day."

Devlin saluted. "Aye aye, Cap'n."

Not only was she sexy as hell, but she was cute as a button.

Olivia turned her attention to me. "You, sir, on the other hand, need to be ready by the crack of ten A.M. for the signing."

"I'm nervous, but excited."

"Don't worry, you'll do great. We put your table right next to mine and Ali's, so if you need anything just let me know."

Honestly, I was completely shocked they'd assigned such a good spot for me. Clearly Val Weston was too, because she let out a low, but audible huff, and her scowl bloomed into an expression of shit-eating disgust.

Olivia ignored Val's pouting and introduced Devlin to the table.

"Everyone, this is Clay's better half, Devlin, she's an artist."

"What kind of art?" Val's nice neighbor asked, which again seemed to agitate Val."

"I'm a tattoo artist," Devlin replied, and Val rolled her eyes in response.

Devlin must have seen her because her tone sharpened as she directed her attention directly to Val.

"Hi, I'm Devlin."

"Valerie," she replied with minimal effort.

"It's nice to meet you. Is this your first reader cruise?"

"Val is an author," I said as pleasantly as possible.

"It's Valerie," she corrected.

Lately, it's become painfully clear to me that that type of correction is the new currency of the passive aggressive. When a person has a shitty attitude and nothing constructive to add to the conversation at hand, they reduce themselves to policing the words of others.

"I'm sorry," I chuckled. "I just assumed since you introduced yourself to me as Val, four minutes ago, that you preferred to be called Val." I looked down at the table to see a stack of books sitting next to her that read VAL WESTON.

"You know what they say about when you assume," she replied.

Devlin squeezed my hand so hard I thought I'd be the next one to need a cast.

"Okay, it's Valerie then. I'll make a note of that for next time."

"Next time we what?" Val replied. "I've never seen you

at any signings, and I have no idea who you are."

"Like I said before, there's no reason you would have, I'm just trying to break into the scene."

The woman sitting opposite Val said, "I've read all three of your books. I think they're great," and got a dirty look from Val in return.

"I've been a Clay Morningwood fan since day one," Olivia said, once again trying to keep the conversation from completely flaming out.

"Morningwood? Seriously? That is by far stupidest pen name I've ever heard of." Val whined.

I laughed uncomfortably and shrugged. What the fuck else was I supposed to do, shove this bitch's face into her Waldorf salad?

"I thought it would be fun. Something that would get people's attention. I treat the craft of writing seriously, but I never want to take *myself* too seriously. I think people will understand."

Val raised an eyebrow. "There ya go makin' assumptions again, and you know what they say—"

Devlin let go of my hand, braced herself on a chairback, and leaned over the table. "I know exactly what they say about making assumptions," she said, her face a stone. "But do *you* know how long a dumb bitch can survive in open waters after being thrown off a cruise ship?"

* * *

Devlin

When I was in the fifth grade I was suspended from school for three days for calling my teacher a dick after he gave me a B- on my pterodactyl diorama. I once set fire to a boyfriend's prized collection of vintage Air Jordan's after he gave one of my rings to a girl he was cheating on me with. My mouth and temper have gotten the best of me many times within my lifetime, but I must admit, this was a bold move, even for me.

Val's jaw hung open. "Excuse me?"

"You heard me, and if I have to repeat myself, it'll be outside on deck... where we'll be closer to the rail."

"Okay, babe, let's find a table," Ropes said, his hand on the small of my back.

"I don't know what your problem is, or who you think you are, but if you ever speak to my boyfriend like that again I will end you," I snapped as Ropes guided me away from the table. I don't know what had come over me, but my need to defend him came on suddenly and violently.

"Okay, where is our waiter? Let's get some drinks up in here," Olivia said, waving one hand in the air, and placing the other on Val's, who still wore a look of shock on her twisted face.

"C'mon baby, it's alright," Ropes said with a chuckle as he led me away from my potential murder victim.

I felt a little lightheaded as Ropes moved me as fast I could hobble, through the crowded dining room. I was still jacked up on adrenaline and had to fight the urge to turn around and put my air cast up her tight ass.

"Who the hell was that?" I ground out.

"Val Weston, or Valerie I guess. I'm confused," Ropes replied.

"How 'bout we just call her Valerial Disease to keep things clear?"

Ropes burst out laughing, drawing the attention of every diner, including Darien and Mack, who then waved us over to their private table.

"Hey there, you two," Darien said cheerily. "Are you spoken for tonight, or can you join us?"

"We'd be honored, of course," Ropes said.

"Honored nothin'," Mack said. "I need someone to hang with that prefers beer to this Kool-aid shit they keep trying to pour me."

"I'm a single malt guy myself," Ropes said.

Mack raised an eyebrow. "Then, by all means, please take a seat."

* * *

Ropes

For the rest of the evening the conversation between the four of us flowed easily from bikes, to philosophy. We talked about everything from Club life, to the life of an artist. There was little not to find in common with Darien and Mack. And I dared to let myself begin to dream of a future like this with Devlin.

Darien was full of great advice and insight about the business. She was very generous with information and I felt like I could trust her implicitly, a feeling I rarely had.

"Can I ask you question about your opinions on another author?" I asked.

"My artistic or personal opinion?"

"Personal."

"Yes, but know that I will be honest, and if our opinions differ and your feelings get hurt, it's not my responsibility."

"Fair enough," I said.

"Who are you asking about?"

"Val Weston."

Darien said nothing but made a gagging motion.

"So, I'm not crazy?" I asked.

"No, she's horrible."

I frowned. "She's hitting lists so she's doing something right. Right?"

"She's doing something alright."

"I haven't read anything by her. Is her writing good?" I asked.

"After the first two books, who knows? No one does."

"What do you mean?" Devlin asked.

"Everything she's released after her first two books have been written by ghost writers."

"That's a thing?" I asked.

"From what I've heard, she's employed several different writers over the years. Sometimes she'll give them a very basic outline, and sometimes nothing at all. I suspect her new series have all been written by the same person as they've

142

been the best books under her brand yet."

"That makes me want to throw up," Devlin said.

"I agree, but she's been able to keep her practices pretty tightly under wraps, but cracks are starting to show."

* * *

I secured the spreader bar to Cherry's ankles, and leaned over her, running my tongue across her bare pussy, dipping inside of her already slick folds.

"Max," she panted out, sliding her hands into my hair.

"No touching," I demanded, and her bottom lip popped out in a perfectly formed pout.

"But—"

"Cherry," I said, trying to keep my arousal out of my voice. "You need a lesson in self-control, baby. It's time you learned."

She cupped her tits and rolled her nipples into tight buds. "Fuck self-control."

"Not an acceptable answer," I admonished and slapped my palm against her pussy.

She squeaked and raised her hips in an effort to press against me.

"Jesus," I hissed, and stood.

She licked her lips and smiled up at me. "You're so hot when you're annoyed..." her eyes traveled down my body, landing on my dick, "... and hard."

I gave her a slow smile, gripping the spreader bar and flipping her onto her stomach. She let out a surprised squeak and I slapped a palm against her ass. "Get that ass up, Cherry. Want to see your pussy."

She repositioned onto all fours, and her red hair cascaded down her back. I slid it to the side so I had full access to her body, then I flattened my palm against her folds, running a finger along her clit. She was soaked. "You stay like this, baby. Hear? You move, and I'm gonna fuckin' tie you down, understand?"

Goosebumps whispered across her skin and she nodded.

143

"I understand," she whispered.

"You do not come until I tell you to come."

"I don't know—"

I pulled my hand away. "You do not come until I tell you to come."

She whimpered, wriggling her ass in the air, before nodding.

I gave her ass a gentle pat, then secured clamps to her nipples, giving the chain a gentle tug. "Too tight?"

She shook her head and I smiled, sliding my hand between her legs and feeling a new rush of wetness. Grabbing the spreader bar, I tugged on it slightly and her legs went out from under her. I guided her legs over the side of the bed, knowing the clamps were pulling on her nipples, but trusted that she'd use our safety word if it was too much.

"Arms out, Cherry."

She spread her arms wide, fingertips to the edge, and I grabbed her vibrator and squeezed lube over the tip. "We're gonna try something new. Trust me?"

She nodded, her gorgeous globe of an ass wriggling like it did when she was trying not to come.

"Good girl," I encouraged.

I placed the tip of the vibrator against her ass. Sliding my dick into her pussy, I guided the vibrator into her tight hole. She whimpered again, pressing back against me and I flipped the toy on. She screamed my name and I sighed.

"I fuckin' told you not to come," I ground out.

"Wait," Devlin said, ceasing her out loud reading and raising her head from the computer. "How often has this chick had something stuck up her ass?"

I shrugged. "Haven't really gone there, baby. Never?"

She raised an eyebrow. "How many times have you stuck your dick into someone's ass?"

"Never," I admitted. She burst out laughing and I crossed my arms. "What the fuck, Devlin?"

"Sorry, sorry," she said, trying to control her giggles. "No, seriously. It's good."

"Yeah, I can tell you think so."

She set the laptop aside and slid off the bed. "Okay, let's break this down, because I'm in a bit of a conundrum."

"Yeah?"

She nodded. "I'm so fucking turned on, but I'm also trying to imagine what it would be like for a woman who's never had anything stuck up her ass not to react in pain."

"It's fantasy, Devlin."

"I understand that, but there should be some form of reality, don't you think? If I'm reading fiction, I don't want to be pulled out of the story if something doesn't hold true. I also really like this Max guy. I'm kind of wondering how to get you to be more like him in bed."

"Excuse me?"

"I'm not complaining," she rushed to say. "I'm just intrigued."

"I happen to respect you, Devlin. And we're new. I wanted to ease you into the kink."

"Oh, I'm in, honey. Kink works for me, if you're into it."

My heart raced and my dick nearly sprang out of my boxers. "What do you suggest?"

She bit her lip and ran her hands down my chest. "I suggest we do some research."

"Yeah?"

She nodded, pulling her T-shirt off, leaving just her panties. "That treasure chest looked like it had some good stuff in there, let's take a look."

I swallowed. "Fuck, seriously?"

Devlin's hand slid under the waistband of my boxers and her fingers wrapped around my dick. "I'm so unbelievably serious right now, you have no idea."

I kissed her quickly, then retrieved the chest so she could find her toy of choice. I was so fucking hard, I thought I might burst out of my skin. But when she held up a bright pink vibrator, handed it to me, and slid her panties off, I knew I was going to have to slow my roll or I'd come all over her ass.

She licked her lips. "All fours, right?"

I nodded, my breath coming in short bursts. "Right."

Devlin knelt on the bed and got onto all fours, her ass in the air as she grinned at me over her shoulder.

I set the vibrator on the bed and stepped out of my boxers, grabbing her hips and running my tongue over her folds. "I swear to God, your pussy gets sweeter every time I taste you."

"Yeah, yeah, let's try the vibrator."

I chuckled, picking up the toy and pressing it inside of her, wetting it with her juices before settling it at the entrance of her ass. I flipped the switch and she pressed back against the vibration.

"Mmm," she moaned.

"Okay?" I asked.

"Yeah, honey. I promise I'll tell you if it isn't working for me, but I want you to play out what you just wrote."

"So, you want me to LARP."

"As long as the 'P' in LARPing stands for 'pussy,' and that vibrator's in my ass, LARP away."

"I don't think Live Action Role Pussy has the same ring to it."

"How about Lubed Ass and Red Pussy," I suggested.

"Oh, let me write that down," I joked.

"Oh my word, Ropes, shove your dick in me right fucking now."

I did as she demanded and grinned when she cried out in ecstasy as I entered her wet pussy.

"Yes, that's it," Devlin cried as I slid the vibrator deeper. She shimmied back and I pushed my cock further inside as I continued working her ass.

"Oh, my..." Devlin rasped.

I held the vibrator steady as I moved, burying myself deeper inside of her, then matching the motion with the vibrator as I fucked her.

It didn't take long before her walls contracted around me and she screamed my name into the bedding. I dropped the vibrator onto the bed so I could focus on slamming into her, my orgasm hitting me like a freight train as I pumped my seed inside of her. As I worked to catch my breath, all I could think about was putting a baby in her belly and making her mine permanently.

Ropes

I DOWNED MY third cup of coffee and turned my attention back to sorting through my boxes of inventory while Devlin continued to sleep off last night's debauchery. I don't know why I'd brought so many books with me. It was likely I'd end up hauling most of them back home with me. In fact, the more I thought about it, the more I wondered why I'd ever agreed to this signing anyway. Val Weston was right. Who the fuck was I? A nobody, that's who. A greenhorn author with a couple of books under his belt, and a few sales on Amazon. I began pacing the floor of our cramped quarters, and Devlin stirred.

"You okay?" she asked, wiping her eyes.

"Sorry to wake you. Go back to bed, baby. I'll be quieter."

She sat up and shook her head. "Tell me. You look freaked."

"I'm okay, just wondering if I could hotwire one of those lifeboats and sail back to Portland before I make a complete fool of myself."

"What are you talking about? Everyone loved you last night," she said.

"I'm sure they were just being nice."

Devlin sighed. "Can I ask you a serious question?"

"Sure."

"What the fuck is wrong with you?"

"What?" I asked, taken aback by her question.

"I'm serious." She tapped a temple with her fingers. "Have you ever been tested for a mental defect?"

"Come on, Devlin. This boat is full of legitimate authors. Writers who make their living from what they do. I'm just a biker who's posing as a writer."

"That's bullshit, and you know it. You may also be a biker, but you are most certainly a *legitimate* author. I've been reading your books since we got on this tub, and you, sir, can write."

I shrugged. "Maybe, but that doesn't guarantee anybody will buy my books today."

She pushed up to her knees and motioned me closer. "True, great writing doesn't guarantee book sales, but you obviously felt confident enough to sell this business idea to Minus. You must have some confidence in what you're doing."

"I guess."

I stood in front of her and she slid her hands up my chest. "You must have made some sales since you started publishing."

"Sure, enough to cover my monthly nut and put a little in the bank," I revealed.

"That's amazing, Ropes. Do you know how many artists never see a dime for their efforts, let alone cover their monthly bills?"

"It's not like my overhead is very high. I live at the Sanctuary, and my bike and truck are paid off. Plus, I've made investments and have a little money of my own."

"Even still, you shouldn't ignore the fact that you've made a positive entrance into the writing world or minimize where all of this could take you. Besides, I heard you talking with some of the other authors last night, and it sounds like everyone on the boat is at various levels of their careers."

"Maybe, but Ali said she assigned me to a great table."

"I would think that's a good thing, but you're making it sound like a bad thing."

"I just don't know why she'd do that."

Devlin wove her fingers into my hair. "I think maybe you're overthinking all of this. You're going to do great. I believe in you and will be right there by your side the whole time." She leaned in for a kiss, pressing her naked body against mine.

"You keep doing that and we'll never make it out of our cabin."

She wrinkled her nose in disappointment. "Then get in the shower, because your public awaits, Mr. Morningwood."

* * *

Devlin

Ropes pushed my carriage, aka, a wobbly-wheeled luggage cart, through what felt like miles of narrow hallways, up the elevator, and through the maze that was the ship's casino, until we reached our destination: the Royal Ballroom. The cart was half-filled with boxes of books and swag, and half-filed with Devlin the one-legged assistant. I couldn't wait to get rid of this stupid boot. It slowed down everything I had to accomplish, and it robbed me of sexy points I desperately needed right now. Some of the women on this cruise were drop-dead-gorgeous and they were looking at my man like he was gonna be their next snack.

"Damn, I'm already a sweaty mess," he said as the cart rolled to a stop.

"Are you saying I'm heavy?" I asked.

"Oh, shit, baby... I—"

"Sweetie, I'm teasing. Relax, I promise everything's going to be okay."

"I'm telling you, this sweat is from nerves. I'll run back to the cabin and change before the signing."

"I'll go and get you a change of clothes," I said. "I'm afraid you'll run off and hide in the cabin."

"With your boot, you'd get back just in time for the after party."

"Just find your table, *Clay.*"

He rolled us to the first row of tables and stopped suddenly. "Holy shit!" he exclaimed, his voice booming through the mostly empty ballroom.

"What?" I asked, while giving him the universal hand gesture for 'lower your fucking voice you lunatic.'

"Baby, they've put me on 'Murderer's Row.'" Ropes gestured wildly. "Olivia's table is there, and I'm right between Ali, and D.W."

"Wow, you weren't kidding when you said Ali hooked you up with a good spot."

"I'm gonna throw up."

"Again, I must remind you this is a good thing."

"I need to start setting up," Ropes said, frantically pawing at the stack of boxes.

"It's okay, babe, you've got plenty of time. People are just starting to get set up."

"I've got to do something to keep my mind off all this," he said, staring forward blankly.

"Tell you what," I said. "I'm gonna go hobble over to the breakfast bar and get us some real coffee, okay? Whatever that was back in our cabin didn't get nearly enough caffeine into the bloodstreams of a couple of Portlanders like us, right?"

"Thank you, baby. Coffee sounds great if you think you can manage."

"You've been very sweet, and I've been an enormous baby about this boot. I'm perfectly fine, and I'll be right back with coffee. If you're lucky, maybe they'll have donuts."

"I'd never cheat on Omar." Ropes smiled, and quickly went back to his inventory. It truly was strange to see him so rattled, so... vulnerable. Ropes was a confident biker, who'd bust a man's jaw without hesitation. Clay was a sensitive soul, who was terrified of letting his readers down or making a fool of himself in front of the people he respected most.

In the end I knew both Ropes and Clay Morningwood were both manifestations created by Spencer Kimble. A lost boy in a cruel world. I only hoped I was up to the task of handling all three of them.

I made my way to the breakfast bar and found a beautiful buffet with everything from eggs to Eggos. One of the beautiful curses of a cruise ship, as I would come to find, is the endless supply of food. Everything from gourmet dining to pure junk food. If it could fit in my mouth, apparently, it was on this boat.

I poured two cups of coffee and loaded mine up with non-caloric rat poison. After looking down at my bloated stomach, I also decided to forgo my usual splash of cream. I'd only been on the boat for a night, and I was convinced I'd already gained five pounds. I scanned the buffet for a healthy option for me and something wicked for Ropes. That skinny bastard was gonna match me pound for pound gained while on this tub if it killed me.

"Excuse me," a quiet voice from behind me said, causing me to jump and spill my coffee a little. "Oh, my gosh. I'm so sorry," a mousy woman wearing glasses said, handing me a stack of napkins from the silverware station."

"It's okay, you just scared me a little," I said, wiping my hands. "Did you need to get by me?"

"Oh, no," She said, her eyes darting between me and the floor. "I wanted to talk to you. Your name is Devlin, right?"

"That's right. What's your name?"

"I'm Norma Pickler."

"Nice to meet you, Norma." I extended my hand which she took timidly. I'm not sure what we did could legally be considered a handshake given its extreme brevity, but Norma seemed sweet, and very shy.

She continued, her voice barely above a whisper. "I was at the table last night with Val Weston." She paused and gave me an odd smile.

"Oh," I said, my voice dropping an octave.

"Yeah, well, I just wanted to apologize for how she was treating Clay... and you, last night."

"You have nothing to apologize for, Norma. If whatever-her-name-is Weston has a problem with Clay, she can bring it up with him. If she has a problem with me, she should keep walking, for her own good."

"I understand, but I've known her for a while now and she's quite nice once you get to know her. It's just that sometimes her strong personality gets her into trouble."

"More like her bitchy resting face coupled with her bitchy waking face." The words flew out of my mouth before I could contain them.

Norma's face dropped, and I began to sweat. I had no idea who this woman was, she could be some sort of literary big shot for all I know. I began to spiral. Clay was probably Norma's favorite author and I just slammed her friend. I stood frozen in fear, watching Norma's stunned expression for a period that felt longer than the muster station drill. Suddenly, Norma broke the awkward silence by bursting out in laughter. The size of her laughter did not match the size of her body, and I thought she might pass out from her utter lack of inhaling.

"Bitchy... alert... face..." she howled, tears streaming down her face. After a minute, she was able to compose herself enough to continue. "Anyway, I just wanted to say I was sorry for the way Val treated you both. You seem like very nice people. I've read all of Clay's books, and I enjoyed them very much," she said sweetly before turning away.

"Well, come tell him yourself. Clay is getting everything set up now. Come by table number three in a little bit. I'm sure he'd love to meet you."

"Oh, I don't think... no... I don't want to bother... oh... no," she said before beating a hasty retreat down the nearest row of tables.

"It was nice meeting... you," I called out to the timid tornado that was Norma Pickler.

* * *

Ropes

By the time Devlin returned with our breakfast I'd had time to collect myself. I'd sorted through my thoughts as I sorted books, and by the time my table display was ready, I was excited for the signing to start. That was until I looked around at the behemoth displays the other authors were setting up. They all had trade-show quality banners, runners, and promotional materials. Earlier I was worried that I'd overpacked, and now looking down at my meager display, I had just the opposite fear.

"Oh, my gosh, a reader was just fangirling over you," Devlin said excitedly as she set the food down on my table, which had ample space due to a lack of titles and quality merchandise.

This was a mistake. What am I doing here? I'm a phony.

"Clay... Clay... Ropes!" Devlin whisper shouted, and I snapped to attention.

"What?"

"Did you hear what I said? You were kinda zoned out there."

"Yeah, uh, sorry," I said, taking a second to mentally hit the rewind button. "Something about someone fangirling?"

"Yes, over you," Devlin said with a playful smile and poke in my ribs. "Or should I say, over Clay."

"No way, I'm sure she was just being nice. Who was she?"

"Her name is Norma, and she's friends with Val Weston."

"And she was *nice?*"

"I know, right? She came up to me while I was getting coffee to apologize for Val being a complete vag-hat to you."

"She didn't say that."

"Not in so many words, but she was very sweet, and thought I was hilarious when I called Val a bitch."

"Oh, now I see why you liked her so much."

"Shut up, writer boy. Anyway, I invited her to come meet you and she had a stroke and ran away."

"You're out of your mind."

"I'm not even exaggerating."

I changed the subject back to the current object of my neurosis, my table.

I placed my hands upon Devlin's shoulders and looked deeply into her eyes. "Forget about all that. I need you to help me."

"What can I do?"

"Kill me and throw my body overboard."

"But if you're not here to sell the books, how will you make money for the club?" Devlin deadpanned.

"They can have my life insurance policy," I replied.

"You have a life insurance policy? Oh, right. Rich kid," Devlin teased.

"Ex-rich kid, current nervous wreck."

"You're going to be fine," she tried to reassure me.

"That's what I'm worried about. Being just *fine*. Look at some of these tables, Devlin. These authors have way more titles and experience. I don't want to look like an imposter next to them. This is hard for me. When I'm with my club I know who I am, but now that I'm here I feel like an imposter.

Devlin took my face in her hands. "You're not an imposter, you're an author. An author with a small, but growing fanbase of wonderful readers, who have spent their time and money to come on this boat to meet you. They came to see you, Clay Morningwood, not your table. They fell in love with your words, and the man that wrote them. I know how they feel because I did too, so just show these readers your heart today and you'll do great.

I leaned down and kissed her slowly. "You know, if you're ever ready to hang up your tattoo gun, you'd make a hell of a motivational speaker."

* * *

"Say it!" Devlin yelled as she rained down her assault from above.

"I'll never tap out," I replied and held her wrists as she wriggled and squirmed to break free of my grasp.

"Say it. Say I was right, you jerk."

"I think you're overestimating your position," I challenged, not wanting to show Devlin how exhausted I truly was.

"Oh, yeah?" Devlin quickly slid her knee between my legs up to my crotch.

"Hey, no low blows," I said, and rolled Devlin onto her back.

"No fair," she protested, and I kissed her neck as she continued to squirm.

"Say I was right."

"Okay, now I know you don't understand the rules of wrestling. You don't make demands while you're losing."

"You're the loser," Devlin teased.

"Not today," I exclaimed triumphantly, letting go of Devlin to strike a flex pose.

"That's right, and it's all because of who?"

"Because of you," I said in mock surrender.

"Because why?"

"Because... you were right."

"That's right, motherfuckers," Devlin yelled jubilantly. "Clay Morningwood rocked his first signing and sold out."

"That's not true, I still have eight books left," I corrected.

"Close enough," she said, "Now pour me another glass of that fancy-ass Champagne, and since we're on a boat, why don't you fuck me like one of your French whores, Jack?"

I chuckled. "I think you may need to watch Titanic again. I'm not quite sure that's exactly what Kate Winslet said."

I felt a mixture of elation and exhaustion, something I hadn't felt since my early days as a full patch in the Saints, during my first long runs to Idaho and California. The signing had gone better than I could have possibly imagined, and I felt like I'd used every muscle in my body today, including ones inside my brain I never knew existed.

"I can hear you thinking, and you should be fucking," Devlin said, snapping my full attention back to her. She was so fuckin' sexy, and despite my exhaustion, I couldn't wait to bury myself inside of her.

"Sorry, it's been one hell of day," I said, my voice sounding like it did back when I still smoked.

"I can take a rain check if you're too tired, or you can hand me the treasure chest and I'll find something to take care of myself with."

"I'll always take care of you," I said, and pulled off my shirt.

* * *

Devlin

"Where do you want me?" Ropes asked, and I took a moment to decide what I wanted to do to him.

"Stand in front of the bed," I said.

I sat on the edge, unable to kneel due to my boot, and wrapped my hand around his already hard shaft. "I wish I had red lipstick," I mused as I slid my mouth over his tip.

His sharp intake of breath made me smile, but then I was all about how quickly I could make him come, and I took him deeper, moving my hand with the motion of my mouth, faster and faster before gripping his ass and encouraging him to fuck me back.

It didn't take much, then his hands were on my head and he was pulling me forward (not that I needed much encouragement there), and he was fucking my mouth... hard.

"Fuck, Dev, I'm gonna come."

I nodded and the warmth of his cum filled my mouth and I took it all. He pulled out and I found my panties tugged from my body, then he pushed me back and knelt between my legs. His mouth covered my core and he sucked gently, before running his tongue between my folds and sliding his fingers inside of me.

I gripped his hair as he sucked, fingered, and blew me to

a mind-blowing orgasm, this time it was his turn to take my juices into his mouth. Ropes had done his job and I felt taken care of, as promised.

EIGHTEEN

BURNING SAINTS

Devlin

I SMOOTHED MY *extra short, extra tight skirt over my hips and twisted my body to see every angle in my full-length mirror. I wanted to be perfect tonight. Max was* taking me out. It was an unusual event and I wanted more of them, so I took special care to make it worth his time and effort.

Don't get me wrong, I loved our 'sessions.' I would submit to him in any way, on any day, but a session in public made me wet just thinking about it and I wanted to grab my vibrator and give myself some relief. That would be against the rules, however, so I took a few deep breaths and focused on finishing my makeup.

Adding an extra layer of cherry-red lipstick, I pressed my lips together and smiled. Max loved red on me, and I remembered him enjoying the sight of my lipstick on his dick, so my hope was, after seeing my choice of lip color, he would let me suck him off again tonight.

I'd chosen to go completely bare tonight, but I took a pair of panties and shoved them into my clutch, just in case I needed some protection. Sitting gingerly on the edge of a chair, I slid on the Louis Vuitton stilettos Max had given me, then rose to my feet just as my doorbell rang.

I shivered in anticipation of the evening and made my way to the door. After checking the peephole, I pulled my door open, lowering my head, and clasping my hands in front of me. "Good evening."

Max's fingers came to my chin and he gently lifted it. "Good evening, my beautiful Cherry. You may look at me."

My eyes met his and the look of burning desire nearly had me sliding to my knees to beg for an orgasm. Just one would do for the moment.

"You look bothered, sweetheart," he observed.

I squeezed my legs together and took a deep breath. "I'm excited, Max."

"Are your panties wet?"

"I'm not wearing panties, Max."

His quiet, quick intake of breath made me smile, but I tried to hide my glee. I wanted him to fuck me and being too pleased with myself often meant straight sex. I didn't want it straight tonight, I wanted it kinky as hell.

His hand slid between my legs and his thumb whispered over my clit. I swallowed and grasped the doorframe as he slipped two fingers inside of me.

"Soaked," he observed.

I nodded.

He smiled slowly, then his fingers moved inside of me, while his thumb added more and more pressure to my clit. I bit my lip and dropped my head back as he finger-fucked me in the doorway of my apartment where anyone could walk past at any time.

"Max," I breathed out.

"Shhh," he whispered.

I bit my lip and gripped the doorframe harder.

"Spread your legs, Cherry."

I did as he demanded and his hand shifted so his palm connected with my mound as he added another finger to my pussy. Then he pumped his fingers into me faster and faster, his palm slapping me as he went, and I knew, just knew, I was going to have to stay silent as I came. This caused both fear and anticipation and my body reacted immediately. I gulped in several deep breaths as I came against his hand and then focused on him as he pulled his hand away, his palm glistening with my juices.

Max ran his tongue over his hand, then sucked his fingers into his mouth and smiled. "Fucking delicious, baby." Settling a finger on my lower lip. "Open." I opened my mouth and he slid his finger into my mouth. "Taste."

I sucked his finger, my lipstick adding a bright red ring to the digit and I hoped once again he'd let me do the same to his dick later.

He pulled his hand away, took a handkerchief from his pocket, and wiped his hand as he grinned, then slid the linen between my legs to clean me up. "Good girl. Are you ready?"

I nodded, smoothing my skirt down and grabbing my keys. I handed them to him and he locked up, helping me down the stairs and to the awaiting car.

"Holy crap," I breathed out. I was sitting on the top deck of the ship, lounging on a chaise while Ropes took a dip in the pool. I could feel my bikini bottoms dampen as I read another excerpt from Ropes's current manuscript.

Ropes glanced at me from the middle of the pool and I squeezed my eyes shut slightly and took a deep breath.

"You okay?"

I squeaked and opened my eyes, which were shaded behind dark sunglasses, cold water dripping onto me as Ropes wrapped a towel around his waist.

"No," I admitted.

"Your foot bothering you?" he asked in concern.

I shook my head. "Not my foot."

"Well, what's wrong, then?"

I shifted in my seat. "I decided to read a little more of your story, *Clay*, that's what's wrong. And now I'm horny as fuck, sitting on a lounge chair in the open air, when all I want to do is drag you somewhere and continue what we started last night."

"Holy shit," he hissed. "Let's find someplace right now."

"I'd love to, be we don't have that much time. We've gotta get back to the cabin and change for the end-of-cruise party."

"When's that?"

"Not until the evening."

"Babe, it's kind of the evening *now*," Ropes motioned to the sky.

I ripped my sunglasses from my head and gasped to find the sun was setting. I checked my watch and squeaked, "Shit, we're late!"

"It's no big deal," Ropes replied, "We'll just blame your boot."

"It's your fault," I growled. "I lost track of time reading your stupid book."

"Hey," Ropes protested. "I know the guy who wrote that."

"Stop joking around and help me," I snapped.

"It's okay, baby. We can be a little late. Where's the party?" Ropes asked, helping me up.

"In the Skylight Lounge, and we need to be on time." My panic level was starting to rise, as was my irritation with Ropes's cavalier attitude. I hated being late. I had to be where I was supposed to be, when I was supposed to be there. Being late for anything triggered thoughts and feelings about my capture. When I was being held, I had hours, sometimes days to do nothing but think. I started to obsess on thoughts about the outside world moving on without me. I was convinced that no one knew we were missing, and that we'd never be found. Since the rescue, being punctual has been a compulsion.

"We'll never make it in time," Ropes said, casually.

"No shit, Captain Obvious," I snapped.

"Whoa, what did I say?"

"Forget it," I said, frantically stuffing my last belonging into my bag.

"Devlin," Ropes said, grabbing my shoulders. "What's going on? A minute ago, you wanted to jump my bones, and now you're freaking out on me."

"We don't have time for this. We're already late and it's going to take me forever to get back to the cabin with this goddamned boot and my goddamned foot!"

* * *

Ropes

I thought I'd seen Devlin angry when we were alone in Sally Anne's office, but I knew her well enough now to know that was only foreplay. Devlin dropping god bombs made it clear that *now* she was angry. I had no idea why, other than being late, but to me that was more of a minor irritation than anything. Given our current location and the fact that we were late to a cocktail party also made me feel like Devlin was blowing this way out of proportion. However, I was smart enough to keep these thoughts to myself and set my mind to getting Devlin back to the cabin as quickly as possible.

Devlin was silent except for the occasional whimper of pain as we hustled back to the cabin. Any time I'd offer to get her a wheelchair, or take a break, she'd merely grunt at me through pursed lips as she hobbled along. The only bright spot in all of this was seeing Devlin, in her bikini, with a little extra bounce in her step as we walked. In her haste, she didn't even grab a towel when we left the pool. Her perfect alabaster skin accentuated by her beautiful artwork on display for all. Normally I'd be a little jealous, but all I wanted to do was stare at the movement of her incredible body. I took mental snapshots as we walked and stored them away for scene inspiration later.

Devlin finally broke her silence when we got to our cabin. "Do you have the room key?"

"I thought you had it," I replied.

"What?"

"I was wondering where you were hiding it the whole time we were walking here."

Devlin scowled at me and I produced the card key from my shorts pocket with a grin.

"Not funny," she said as she scooted past me into the room.

* * *

Devlin

I took one of my last remaining pain pills and washed it down with what was left in last night's Champaign bottle. Both my toe and head were throbbing, and I couldn't believe we had to turn around and walk all the way to the lounge. Of course, I could just let Ropes get me a damned wheelchair, but the thought of that was somehow worse.

The Do Not Disturb sign had been on the door all day long so the cabin was a disaster, much like me. We'd spent most of the day by the pool and my windswept hair and makeup-free face showed it. I pulled my hair up as fashionably as possible and put on enough makeup to prevent me from being mistaken as a corpse. The entire cruise had been casual dress, and I'd showed up overdressed to every event thus far, so this time I put on some tight black jeans and a shirt from Fat Donny's and was ready to go. I looked like a lukewarm mess, but I was ready.

Ropes, of course, simply changed from one designer t-shirt to another, ran his fingers through his hair once or twice and looked like he was ready for a modeling shoot.

"Let's go," I said sharply, turning for the door.

"No," Ropes replied.

"We're late enough as it is and you keeping screwing around."

"I'm not screwing around baby, sit down for just a minute so we can talk," he said softly.

I flopped down on the edge of the bed with an aggravated huff.

"I'm sorry for whatever I did that set you off at the pool, and for making us late, and for the Vietnam War if it gets us back on the same page and having fun again."

His obvious sincerity melted my ice-queen heart and I found myself instantly unable to stay mad at him. Besides, I knew he didn't do anything wrong. "I have a thing about being late. It's a big thing actually."

"Okay." Ropes smiled, taking my hands in his. "I can appreciate punctuality."

"It's more than that. Being late, or deviating from plans, triggers feelings of being taken."

"Shit, Devlin. I'm sorry I was clowning around so much, I was just trying to cheer you up."

"I understand, I really do. You didn't do anything wrong, and I should have told you about my anxiety. It's not just being late, there are a lot of things that can trigger my attacks. I'm usually able to keep things together, but sometimes I feel overwhelmed and sort of cave in."

"You can always tell me how you're feeling, no matter what. If I upset you, I want you to tell me, and if you are ever feeling an anxiety attack coming on, you let me know and I'll do whatever you need me to do until it's passed."

I kissed Ropes and burrowed into his chest. He wrapped his arms around me and once again, I felt safe.

NINETEEN

BURNING SAINTS

Ropes

B Y THE TIME we reached the Skylight Lounge, we were twenty-five minutes late to the party, but Devlin's mood had lightened significantly. We were already making jokes about her losing track of time while reading and how much of a bad influence my writing was on her. We made pretty good time from the cabin as Devlin was able to navigate much easier wearing sneakers instead of whatever stylish hell she's usually got strapped to her good foot. We were both looking forward to just hanging at the bar tonight with readers, drinking too much, and crashing now that all the excitement was over.

I opened the heavy lounge doors and every eye in the room turned to look at us.

"There they are!" Olivia announced cheerily into a microphone.

She and Ali were standing on stage, along with Father Finn and several authors including Val Weston. The Authors were all holding large, phallic trophies. Val's read "Best New Release."

"Come on up you two," Olivia said into the mic, waving Devlin and me to the stage.

Devlin quickly took my hand and squeezed tightly. "I'm going to kill you," she said quietly while smiling to the crowd of attendees.

Everyone in the room was dressed in cocktail attire. Everyone except for us of course. I'd somehow missed the memo that this was a formal gathering and knew right away that Devlin's good mood was likely considerably less so right about now.

"I'm sorry," I muttered back, but she only squeezed my hand tighter. I led her up the steps to the stage and over to Olivia and Ali.

"Here they are, your Books and Booze Cruise 'Cutest Couple,'" Olivia said.

"Wait, what?" Devlin asked.

"The last night of the cruise is always awards night. The readers cast their ballots today at lunch."

"The people have voted," Ali said. "It was damned near unanimous. You two are a-fuckin'-dorable."

The room filled with cheers and awes and Devlin and I shared a shocked look. Father Finn presented us with our major award as Olivia thrust the mic in my face and I blurted out the most intelligent thing I could muster, "Um, thanks."

Olivia began to move the mic to Devlin, who pursed her lips tightly and shook her head. Wisely, Olivia took the cue and backed off.

We turned to exit the stage and the crowd began to chant, "Kiss, kiss, kiss." I smiled at Devlin, and she began to laugh nervously, cracking from the absurdity of it all. I leaned down and kissed her softly.

Devlin leaned in and whispered, "You'll pay for this,

writer boy."

I'm paying right now.

I smiled at the crowd and yelled out, "Thank you," before turning to lead Devlin to the stairs.

"Hold on, you two," Olivia said before we could make our retreat. "You may as well stay up here for the next award."

"This is a really special award for us," Ali said. "As the event coordinators, we're not eligible to vote, but I'll be honest, if we could have, we would have voted the same as you. Ladies and gentlemen, we'd like to present this year's rising star award to Clay Morningwood."

I stood there stunned, a buzzing in my ears building up as Ali continued.

"Each cruise, the readers get to vote on the author whose work they are most excited to read in the future. Once again, it was a landslide. What can we say, Clay? They love you and we love you."

I think I managed to smile, but the buzzing in my head was getting louder and the room began to spin. I tried to focus on Olivia and Ali, and managed to choke out, "Thank you," and "excuse me," before jumping from the stage and bolting to the nearest exit.

I ran out of the room, leaving Devlin standing on stage with the others, a golden dong in each hand. I left through a side exit that led directly to the ship's starboard deck. I moved briskly until I reached the ship's rail. I took in several deep breaths, filling my lungs with fresh, salty ocean air.

What the fuck is wrong with you? Pull it together.

I wondered if this was what Devlin felt like when she had a panic attack.

Shit, is that what's happening to me?

I leaned over the edge as far as I could, breathing deeply and fighting back the urge to hurl over the side of the boat.

"Baby are you okay?" Devlin's sweet voice rang out.

I turned to see Devlin's beautiful frame, walking toward me, silhouetted in the breaking moonlight.

"I'm okay. I just needed some fresh air. I was feeling a

little… I don't know… overwhelmed I guess."

"I get it,'" Devlin said, putting her hand to my face. "Oh, my gosh. You're burning up."

"Just a little overheated, I'll be fine."

"We were all worried. You looked like you'd seen a ghost."

"More like the ghost of my own future," I replied.

"What do you mean?"

"Until recently, my life was simple, and I had a pretty good idea of where I'd be in ten years. Now when I look into the future all I see is chaos and uncertainty."

"I sure hope you don't see me as a part of that chaos," Devlin replied.

"Actually, I do, and that's part of the problem."

"Now I'm chaos and a problem?" Devlin took a step backward.

"That's not what I meant."

"You know, for a writer, you can be pretty shitty with words sometimes."

"You're right. I'm sorry. That's exactly why I am a writer. I can take all the time I need choosing precisely the right words to use. I can re-write lines and move dialogue around until everything flows just right."

"Then what did you mean by 'chaos and uncertainty'?"

"When I was Spencer Kimble, I never thought about the future. It would all be planned out by my family and a team of lawyers anyway so what was the point. As Ropes, soldier for the Burning Saints MC, the future was optional. As a one percenter, I could die on any given day, in any manner. It was a simple fact of life."

"And now?"

"Now? Now I have shit I truly care about. People I love even more than my club. I have writing, I have my brother. I have all these people, and their expectations, but most of all Devlin, I have you, and now that I do, I'm terrified of losing you. I don't want to lose any of this."

"Why would you?" Devlin asked, drawing close to me again.

"Because I don't know how to feel otherwise. To my family, I was a traitor. To the streets, I'm a nobody. To my club, I'm a soldier. Now, I'm trying to do something great with my life. I think with you by my side, maybe I can."

"Then what's the problem?"

"The problem is, now that you're in my life, I don't think I can do any of this without you. I didn't start writing for attention or accolades. I didn't even start writing to become an author. I just did it because I was stuck in county lockup with a pencil, a yellow pad, and a tattered copy of D.W. Foxblood's first MC book. I wrote because I was compelled to write. Just like when I met you, I was compelled to be with you. I told you, Devlin. You're my muse."

"I'm by your side. I'm not going anywhere," Devlin tried her best to reassure me.

"For now. But I know club life, and I have a feeling that things are about to get a lot crazier for the Burning Saints. After this signing I also know that I have a long way to go before my writing and my business is where I want it to be."

"What does that all have to do with me?"

"That's what I'm freaking out about. I don't know where you fit, because I don't want to fit you anywhere."

"Are you breaking up with me?"

"Fuck me, Devlin. No." I put my hands on her shoulders. "What I mean is, I know you have your own plans and your own life, and I can't expect you to be by my side through every aspect of my schizophrenic, weird-ass, fucked up life."

"How about you let me decide exactly what I do and don't want to be involved with," Devlin said and pulled me in for a kiss. "We'll figure all of this out. We have time."

I wanted to believe her but felt a sense of dread.

"I love you, Devlin and don't want to see you get hurt again. You've been through enough shit and I'd ride off the Burnside Bridge if my lifestyle somehow put you through more."

"If you ride off that bridge, honey, I'll be at your back."

"Yeah?"

She grinned. "Always."

I kissed her slowly and once again dared to dream of a secure future with her.

"Should we go back to the party?" she asked.

"Yes, but I'd rather take a walk under this beautiful sky with an even more beautiful woman," I said.

"Good answer."

We strolled along the ship's deck, arm in arm for around a half an hour, talking, stopping occasionally to look out at the vast black sea. A sea that mirrored our future, full of possibilities and mysteries. Deep and vast, yet at the mercy of the changing winds. We stopped at an outdoor bar and had a few Captain Blue Breezes which we'd come to find were as advertised, strong and tasty.

"You ready to call it a night?" I asked, catching Devlin mid-yawn.

"No, I'm not," she said defiantly. "This is our last night at sea, and I'm not ready to be Land Devlin again."

"Land Devlin?" I chuckled.

"Sure," she slurred slightly. "If you can be Clay Morningwood I should get to have a super-secret code name as well. At least while I'm on the boat."

"But we're only on the boat for a few more hours."

"Then time's a wastin', pal. You'd better give me a name."

"Speaking of wasted," I said mockingly under my breath.

"What did you say Clay Yummywood?"

"Nothing, dear. I'm just thinking of your name."

"That's what I thought."

"Okay, I've got it," I exclaimed triumphantly. "You are hereby, and for the duration of this cruise, to be known as 'Lady Jubilee.'"

Devlin squealed, "I love it," and threw her arms around me.

I motioned to the bartender for another round and from behind us heard "Oh, god, these two again." I spun around to see Val Weston walking with three of her posse. Devlin must have heard her as well because the next thing I knew she was on her feet and in Val's face.

"What did you just say?"

"What's the matter?" Val asked "Didn't you and your phony boyfriend get enough stage time already tonight? Now you have to come out here and draw attention."

"What the hell are you talking about, you crazy bitch? We're sitting here at the bar having a drink... wait a minute, did you just call him a phony?"

"He knows he is. I don't know who he slept with to get on the cruise, but I'd never heard of him before. Honestly, now that I have, I don't see anything special about him or his writing."

There had now been two times when I thought I'd seen Devlin angry. I was more wrong than I possibly could have imagined.

"First of all, I am Lady Jubilee and I will cut a bitch. Secondly, you are the last person on the planet to call any writer aboard this cruise, a phony."

By now, Olivia, Ali and a small crowd of cruisers had gathered around the bar.

"Neither of you have any business being here or any-where within this industry and you both know it."

"Say that again, and I promise I will commit a maritime crime," Devlin warned.

"Okay, ladies, maybe it's time to go to our cabins," I said, inserting myself between what could become tonight's main event.

"You're so tough with your big, bad, fake boyfriend around, aren't you?" Val challenged, and Devlin lunged with ill intent, her forward momentum halted by an ear-piercing screech.

"Stop it! Just stop it right now!"

I looked down to see a woman who looked to be in her late forties, with a light brown, page-boy haircut, wearing a sweater. I recognized her as the one reader at Val's table that said she'd read my work.

"Norma?" Devlin asked, puzzled.

"Just stop it, Val. I've had enough of your bitch resting awake face," she yelled before turning to Devlin and flashing her a thumbs up.

"Norma, you'll be quiet if you're smart," Val seethed.

"I'm not smart, Val. If I were smart, I would have never gone into business with you in the first place."

"Shut up, Norma."

"I should have never agreed to be your latest ghost writer."

Gasps and murmurs rippled through the crowd.

"Daaaaayummm, Norma," Lady Jubilee shouted.

"You're in breach of contract and you'll be hearing from my lawyer," was Val's only response, before turning on her heels and beating a hasty retreat.

Olivia and Ali came up to us and tears came to Devlin's eyes. "I'm so sorry to both of you. Clay had nothing to do with this, please don't be upset with him, it was all my fault."

"No, it wasn't," Ali said. "It was all Val's fault, and you'll never have to worry about running into her on a Books and Booze Cruise ever again."

"So, Clay is still invited back?"

"Of course," Olivia said, before giving Devlin a big hug. "You both are. Any time."

I kissed Devlin and the group of us proceeded to drink way more than we should have, but that Blue Breeze was a smooth sailin' Captain. It was a perfect end to a crazy night.

TWENTY

BURNING SAINTS

Ropes

THE FLIGHT HOME was a mirror image of the trip to Florida. Devlin and I bickered about everything from armrest etiquette to world politics. We were both hung over and I was pretty sure I was getting sick. I'm sure the tension between us was ninety percent my fault, but I didn't know how to get out from underneath the dark cloud I felt hovering above me. By the end of the cruise I felt confident as an author and as a boyfriend. Now that we were headed home, I felt like a fraud and was convinced Devlin was looking for an exit door as we spoke. To top it off, everything about this flight had ranged from irritating to "stabby," as Devlin would say.

"Here she comes," Devlin said, motioning to the flight

attendant walking toward us.

"Thank God," I said, not bothering to correct myself. Maybe everything I was feeling was related to the burning hunger pangs in my stomach. I'd barely had an appetite while on the boat, but now my body was telling me it needed fuel, big time. I knew if I didn't get some protein in me quickly, this hunger was gonna turn into full blown hanger. Finally, our flight attendant responded to the call button which was pressed only eleven short minutes ago.

"Mmmhmm," was all she said when she arrived at our row, barely making eye contact.

"Good morning," I said as cheerily as possible given my current agitated state. "I didn't quite catch the announcement earlier about the in-flight food service." As if on cue, the baby seated in the row behind us began wailing again.

Our flight attendant delivered a second, "Mmmhmm," with even less enthusiasm than the first.

I forced a smile and continued. "So, I was wondering if you have some sort of meat and cheese plate available."

"All of the food items available for purchase on this flight are located in the in-flight magazine which is located in *every* seat pocket," she said in an irritated monotone voice.

I quickly reached for the magazine in question, flipped to the menu page, and immediately spotted what I wanted. "Great, I'll have two deli packs please," I said, turning to Devlin to see if she wanted to place an order.

"We don't have that on this flight today, sir," the attendant interrupted.

"Oh, okay. I'll take the breakfast sandwich then," I said, the irritation in my voice beginning to creep out.

"Sir," she said sharply. "Breakfast is only served until ten A.M., and it's almost eleven, local time."

"The turkey club then." I said flatly.

"We don't have—"

"So, nothing in the magazine then? Thank you, I'll just eat the free pretzels and maybe my napkin if I'm still hungry."

With that, our corporate appointed Skybitch walked away.

I turned to Devlin. "I'm sorry, did you want to order something from the imaginary kitchen?"

She raised an eyebrow. "You have rage issues."

"I'm sorry," I said, taking her hands. "I'm starving, and it's stupid shit like that that makes me glad I don't have access to the nuclear missile launch codes."

"That's dark."

"I'm serious. The lack of common sense and common decency in the world is driving me crazy."

"Says the outlaw biker," she mused.

"Reformed," I corrected, with a smile.

"Oh, *there* he is," Devlin's face brightened up. "There's the man I fell in love with," she said, reaching into her purse before pulling out a Dr. Fantastic bar.

"Have you been holding out on me this entire time?" I asked. "Hand it over."

"Not so fast," she teased, yanking the candy bar back. "I'll split this with you *if* you agree to be nicer to me."

"Nicer to you?" I protested. "You've been the one nagging at me the whole day."

"Only because, you've been a raging asshole since we woke up," she fired back, her tone less playful.

"What are you talking about? I woke up in a great mood. You were the one that started in on me…"

And so on, and so on, and so on. We bickered over which one of us was being a bigger asshole the entire flight, on the car ride, and then once we arrived back at her apartment. The bickering escalated into arguing, and before I knew it, we were in a full-on fight.

* * *

Devlin

"How did I not see this before?" I snapped.

"What?"

"How big of an asshole you are," I seethed.

"Oh, that's rich coming from you."

"Excuse me?"

He crossed his arms. "You've been ridin' my ass from the second we walked onto that plane. You bitched about the fact I didn't put the carryon in the overhead bin correctly."

"Everyone knows you put the wheels in first! Jebus, were you raised by wolves?"

Ropes dragged his hands down his face and I tried to keep myself from completely melting down. We'd been at each other the entire way home, mostly because he was acting like he was on his fucking period.

"Maybe I should just go."

"Maybe you should," I hissed. "I don't even care if the door hits you on the ass on your way out."

Without another word, he walked out my front door and pulled it shut with a slam. I deadbolted it, then fell onto the sofa in a puddle of frustrated tears. We'd had the best week of our lives and everything had fallen apart the second we'd gotten off the boat. It was becoming evident to me that we might not be cut out for this and that rocked me to my core.

I allowed myself twenty minutes to enjoy a private pity party and then decided it was time to haul my ass off the couch and do some laundry. I had a client at the tattoo parlor in the morning and then a late shift at Sally Anne's. I knew my sleep clock was going to be off due to the time difference, so I figured I'd get as much shit done as I could while I still felt somewhat lucid. Plus, I needed to tattoo someone before I crawled out of my skin. Art had always been my escape. My earliest memories are of hiding under the dining room table with paper and crayons. Drawing for hours while my mother was passed out on the couch, or God knows where else.

I threw my suitcase on the bed and started yanking my clothes from it, coming across various bits of memorabilia from the cruise. I sat and thought about everything Ropes and I had already gone through in the short time that we'd been together, and the waterworks started again.

Lordy, I loved this man, but I just couldn't figure out

how to climb out of the pit of irritation we'd both dug. Or how to fill the hole in and never dig one again.

Since I couldn't do anything to fix it presently, I went about getting sorted for tomorrow's grueling schedule.

The problem was, the more I thought about the fight, the angrier I became. I had a feeling we had one more knock-down-drag-out fight on our horizon.

Ropes

WHEN I ARRIVED at the Sanctuary for Church, I was burned out and in a shitty mood. I'd been riding the biggest high while on the boat, and now that I was back on dry land, I felt completely disconnected from the authors and readers that I'd felt so close to all week. I also felt, for the first time, that Devlin and I weren't on the same page. I hated the way we'd left things and knew the conversation at her apartment was far from over. If she still wanted to talk at all.

How the fuck could I expect any woman to deal with my shit, let alone someone who was clearly working through a pile of her own? Why would such an amazing and independent woman put up with a biker *and* author? Especially after the drama on the high seas she'd just been a part of?

As draining as the cruise was, the last thing I wanted to do was put my kutte on and ride to the Sanctuary. Doing so only pulled me further away from the insulated world we'd just been enveloped in, but it was Wednesday, and that meant Church. No matter how tired I was, no matter whatever personal shit I was going through, club business had to come first. As much as I wanted to be Clay Morningwood right now, I needed to be Ropes.

I reached the gate and Little Pecker buzzed me in. Recruits and new patches would rotate security shifts at the Sanctuary, and today must have been his day. I parked my bike and made my way inside to find most of the Portland chapter members already there. I didn't see my Road Captain anywhere and breathed a sigh of relief. The last thing I needed was shit from Wolf. I caught up with Sweet Pea and Clutch for a few minutes before Minus spotted me and motioned me over to him.

"We've been freezing our asses off here and you come waltzing in looking like George fuckin' Hamilton," he said. "How much fuckin' time did you spend by the pool, drinkin' on my dime?"

"The way my ass is dragging right now, that feels like a million years ago."

"How the fuck can you be tired? You just had a week's vacation."

"I wish. Book signings are exhausting. At least, this one was. Honestly though, it was amazing."

"You think you're gonna be able to make a nickel at this?" Minus asked.

"We're going to find out. The signing went well, and I sold out of just about everything and made a lot of great contacts. We may not get rich overnight, but I feel confident about our plan."

"Good. I look forward to hearing more about the cruise later. To be honest with you, I'm also kinda looking forward to the next Clay Morningwood book," Minus said, under his breath.

I laughed. "No shit?"

"You tell anyone and you're a dead man."

"I can keep a secret," I replied.

"That I know, without a doubt," he said, before checking his watch. "Where the fuck are Wolf and Big Pecker?" he growled softly.

"Little Pecker buzzed me in, and usually where you find one Pecker, you find the other."

"Not today. Wolf split early this morning with Big Pecker, Hoss, and Diamond Dan. They've been gone for hours, and no one knows where they are."

"Maybe they're holding open auditions at the Pink Priest," I replied.

Minus suppressed a laugh. "Well, I'm not waiting around anymore. I've gotta get this meeting started, so I'll chew Wolf's ass out later."

Minus called the meeting to order and the officers, sans Wolf, took their seats around the table. The rest of us found our places, and Minus began.

However, 'Good morning Brothers,' was as far as he got, as the roar of pipes caught the attention of everyone in the room. It sounded like at least a dozen bikes passing through the Sanctuary gates, which was very strange since only a few members weren't present when we started. Moreover, the bikes' engines weren't cut once the bikes were inside but continued to rev, beckoning us to come outside, which we did.

Wolf, along with the other MIA Saints, and ten or more members of the Gresham Spiders were seated on their bikes, and they were all wearing Spiders kuttes. Little Pecker, who'd obviously let them through the gates, stepped out to join them and Wolf handed him a kutte before killing the engine of his bike, which the other Spiders then did.

"What the fuck is this, Wolf?" Minus shouted.

"Since you're such a business man these days, I guess you'd call this my formal letter of resignation," Wolf said, sneering.

"You'd have to be literate in order to write a letter,"

Clutch said.

"You'd better tell your fuckin' lap dog to heel before he gets bit," Wolf said with a sneer.

"This isn't how leaving the club works and you know it," Minus growled.

"Maybe not for you or the Saints, but It's working just fine for me. I'm not playing by your rules anymore, Minus, in case you haven't noticed." Wolf extended his arms to the rows of bikers on either side of him.

"How's it gonna work with you wearing both a Spiders' kutte and Saints ink?" Minus asked.

"I've told you before, Minus. If you feel strong enough to come at me with the brand then take your shot, bubba."

"You know I can't just let you walk."

"You can, and you will," Wolf said. "Me, and any Burning Saint that wants to join me."

"Ain't fuckin' happening you piece of shit traitor," Clutch said, as he pulled his piece and leveled it at Wolf's head.

"What *he* said, motherfucker," Warthog said.

"You wanna start a war by killing a chapter President, then go ahead," Wolf replied. "But we both know you're out of the blood business and ill-fuckin'-prepared for battle."

"What do you mean, 'President'?" Minus asked, side-stepping Wolf's other statement.

"Char isn't getting out of the pen anytime soon, and he knows it. He's decided to run the Spiders from inside the joint and he's patching me in as the Gresham Chapter President. He's giving up his local seat in order to take the club national."

"You're making a big mistake by turning traitor, Wolf."

"Who's the fucking traitor, Minus? You and all this corporate bullshit goes against everything the outlaw biker code stands for."

"Does your code include betraying your club and poaching its members?"

"You betrayed this club when you told us how we can and cannot earn. When you and Cutter put forth your little mandate about being law-abiding citizens. I'm doing something you didn't. I'm giving the Burning Saints a choice. A choice to either go along with your candy-ass plan to play it safe, or patch-in with the Spiders, and live like real bikers again."

"I think Minus made himself pretty clear," Clutch said, his gun still pointed at Wolf. "You and your traitor trash need to get the fuck outta here before I put an extra hole in your empty fucking skull."

"Do it, and you're all dead men. The Spiders outnumber the Saints two-to-one, even more with our new recruits. Plus, Minus has made it very clear that the Saints are no longer one-percenters."

"Put your gun away, Clutch," Minus said calmly.

"What the fuck?"

"I mean it. Wolf is right."

"So, we're just gonna let him take our members and ride outta here?"

"You take who you rode in here with and we won't have any trouble today. Tomorrow is another subject entirely," Minus said. "You try to take any more of my members and I'll cut you down myself, and you know I'm not lying."

Wolf laughed. "Tsk, tsk. A president should lead by example, and here you are threatening violence at your first test."

"Don't push me." Minus spat back. "You've made your intentions clear, now let me tell you mine. I'm gonna let you leave the Sanctuary in one piece and you and I can settle this later. Test me further, and I'll let Clutch do what I know he wants to do."

"You're right about one thing, Minus, this ain't over between us. Not by a long fucking shot." Wolf turned his attention to the rest of us, "Last chance to be real men, and ride with a real club." Not a single remaining member so much as flinched.

"Looks like you've got your answer," Minus said.

"And you got my message," Wolf replied. "The Spiders are calling the shots in Portland now, and we're coming for you and your little club of pretenders."

"I thought you were smarter than this, Wolf."

"And I thought you had balls." Wolf started his bike.

He then cranked his bars to move his bike in closer to our line. Wolf stopped directly in front of Sweet Pea, who was four or five Saints down from me. He spoke to my brother for several seconds, and Sweet Pea listened patiently. Due to his distance and the volume of his pipes, I couldn't make out what he said, but I saw my brother smile briefly, drop his head down, and then cold cock Wolf with an uppercut that sent him flying backward off his bike. I immediately ran to my brother and by the time I'd reached him a single blast from something much bigger than Clutch's side arm caused me to hit the dirt, face first.

"Nobody fucking move," I heard Kitty bellow over the ringing in my ears.

I turned my head to see Kitty holding a Barrett .50 cal rifle, the barrel still smoking.

"Get back on your bike or I'll mow you all the fuck down," Kitty shouted. "I ain't patched in with the Saints, and I don't gotta live by their code, but I swear I'll kill you all myself if you don't ride outta here now."

Wolf got to his feet, wiping the blood that was pouring from his mouth, before righting his bike. "You're a dead man," Wolf sneered through his bloody teeth at my brother, who stood seemingly unphased.

Guns on both sides were holstered and the Spiders began to file out of the Sanctuary grounds, with Wolf riding out last in a cloud of dust.

Minus, without taking his eye off the gate as it closed, coolly but firmly said, "Kitty, Sweet Pea, Clutch, and Ropes in my office now. Everyone else, Church is dismissed, lay low until you hear from me."

What the fuck had I done? As far as I could see, I was the only one of these knuckleheads that kept his cool.

We filed into Minus's cramped office and he used what little space he had to slam the door before composing himself.

"I want you all to listen to me very closely, I want every gun you possess in this office by midnight, and I mean every single gun." Kitty began to speak but Minus cut him off. "I'll get to you in a moment. I've already told Ropes that he's being promoted to Treasurer and I'm making it official as of right now."

Sweet Pea gave me a 'what the fuck' look, and I mouthed back 'sorry.'

Clutch congratulated me, and Minus turned his attention to my brother. "Sweet Pea, the Burning Saints no longer require your services as a soldier."

I began to protest, but Clutch gave me a look that shut me up. Minus's eyes darted to me and then back to Sweet Pea, who stood motionless and expressionless.

"See, that's it," Minus said. "Cool, calm, and collected as always. Unlike your hothead brother." Minus motioned toward me. "It makes me wonder what Wolf could have said to make you hit him, knowing full well that it was going to start an all-out war."

Sweet Pea stood like a statue.

"You're out as a soldier, because if we're going to war, I need you as a Road Captain."

Sweet Pea's eyes widened, and my jaw dropped.

Minus continued, "You threw the first punch, so I'm gonna expect you to help get us out of this shit, without spilling blood." He eyeballed everyone in the room. "I mean it, no violence, unless…"

"Unless what?" Clutch asked.

"Unless absolutely fucking necessary, and I'll be the one to say when that is. I mean it." Minus turned to Kitty. "As for the other fucking lunatic, giant in the room, if you weren't officially my problem before, you are now. Consider yourself patched into the Burning Saints. We'll have an official party for all of you once I get my head wrapped around how I'm gonna keep us all alive."

"Wait a fucking minute," Kitty protested. "I didn't ask to be in your club."

"Look, Kitty, if Sweet Pea threw the first punch, you

clearly fired the first shot."

"With a fuckin' tank," Clutch added, with a chuckle.

"Laugh it up, Sergeant, because he's your fuckin' Deputy now," he said before turning back to Kitty. "I appreciate what you did back there, and I think we've done pretty good by you up until now." Kitty nodded. "I know you want back in with the Dogs of Fire, and I respect your path to redemption with them. I won't even stand in your way if they ever invite you to patch over, but for now, you're a Saint, you understand?"

Kitty nodded and he and Minus exchanged a forearm handshake.

Minus sat down at his desk with a heavy thud. "Alright, now get the fuck outta here and let me figure out how to keep us all alive."

TWENTY-TWO

BURNING SAINTS

Devlin

I HUNG UP and went back to pacing and sulking.

'I'll be right there Devlin.'

I screwed up my face as I mocked Ropes's macho bravado. He'd called me to say he wanted to talk about our argument and I told him I wanted some time. He disagreed and said he'd be 'right there.' I didn't want him to be 'right there.' I wanted him to stay away so I could be pissed at him in private.

Who the hell does he think he is?

My attempt to wind myself up again was cut short by three knocks on my door. Ropes had arrived earlier than I'd expected. He must have been speeding like crazy to get here so quickly, another thing I'd have to chew his ass about.

I unlocked the front door and swung it open wildly. "Exactly how fast were you—"

A meaty hand clasped tightly around my throat and a rag was placed over my mouth and nose.

Upon regaining consciousness, I found myself seated on the chair in the corner of my living room. I call it my flu chair because it's the only place I want to be when I'm truly sick. I can spend hours curled up in this overstuffed monstrosity, shit-faced on Thera-Quil (my own completely unregulated and non- doctor recommended mixture of various over the counter cold meds), and binge-watching Twilight Zone episodes. If I was sick enough and medicated enough, I'd pass the time by knitting a horrible scarf or ill-fitting mittens. From the way my head was pounding, and the nausea was threatening to spill, I thought, just for a moment, I was sick and I'd hallucinated being knocked out by a giant biker.

"Wakey, wakey," a deep voice said as I struggled to focus. "How much of that shit did you put on that rag?" he asked.

"The normal amount, I guess. How the fuck should I know?" Another man answered.

"What the fuck do you mean, 'I guess'?"

"Excuse me for not being an expert in knocking out chicks with chloroform. I don't have a problem getting dates."

"Cause you pay for 'em."

"Fuck you, Slammer."

My head turned toward the direction of the second man's voice.

"See? She's fine. She's waking up."

"Good, because I want Juliette awake when Shakespeare gets here."

Who the fuck are these idiots?

I continued to struggle to wake up but noticed I wouldn't need to struggle against restraints. Neither my hands nor feet appeared to be bound.

"Time to wake up," the large man bellowed, close enough to feel his hot, rancid breath on my neck.

Just then, I heard Ropes's voice outside my front door, "Baby, it's me," followed by two loud thumps. My eyes finally opened fully, to see the front door handle turning.

* * *

Ropes

Between the battle at the not-so-fucking-okay corral and the constant bickering with Devlin, I felt like I'd been hit in the head with a blunt object.

"Baby, it's me," I called out as I reached Devlin's door. I knocked before trying the handle. The door was unlocked, so I made my way inside before actually being hit over the head with a blunt object. I stumbled, and spun around, dazed from the blow. I knew Devlin was pissed at me, but I immediately ruled her out as my assailant when I saw Big Pecker coming at me with a baton.

"Bein' sucker punched don't feel too good does it, pussy?" Big Pecker said as I ducked to avoid a wild swing.

Dazed, and bleeding heavily, I staggered back and saw Little Pecker, armed with a stun gun, standing next to a large upholstered chair. Seated in that chair was a semi-lucid Devlin.

"Now that I'm in a real club, I can make you pay," Big Pecker growled. "I'm gonna fuck that pretty-boy face of yours up so bad, your brother won't even recognize you."

"You made a big mistake coming here, Big Pecker." I unsheathed my knife from my belt.

"His name's Slammer now," Little Pecker called out in his best 'badass' voice. "And my name's Flash, 'cuz I'm so fucking fast," he said, performing some sort of air-karate move.

"Shut the fuck up, and watch her," Big Pecker bellowed.

"You touch her, you die," I spat out, keeping my eyes locked on him as we circled one another.

"We're gonna do more than touch her," Big Pecker grinned. "In fact, I've been reading your latest book and I'm personally gonna do everything on page one-nineteen, and

I'm gonna make you watch."

I changed the grip of my blade from one best used for defensive slashing, to one more akin to stabbing and butchering. I was going to take this fucker's heart from his chest.

Big Pecker swung the baton again, this time connecting with the left side of my body, sending me flying. My opponent outweighed me by nearly double, and I knew without a doubt, Eldie would be taping up cracked ribs by the end of the night. It would be nothing compared to what I was gonna do to Big Pecker, if I could manage to get my hands on him. Little did I know that I was about to get my chance as he was momentarily distracted by a blood curdling scream, coming from directly behind him.

Big Pecker spun around to see just what I was seeing, Little Pecker, aka Flash, was standing frozen with both hands to his face due to the nine-inch aluminum knitting needle sticking out of his eye socket.

He was making the worst sound I'd ever heard another man make. It clearly caught Big Pecker off guard as well, not for long, maybe even just a half of a second, but in the heat of combat, these advantageous moments seem to cause time to slow down. I lunged forward with everything I had, exposing my pummeled left flank as I flew toward Big Pecker. My razor-sharp knife plunged easily into his abdomen as soon as it made contact and blood began to spill out onto the hardwood floors.

I scrambled to my feet, as Big Pecker frantically pressed the deep wound as blood continued to flow. I'd clearly hit a major organ and Big Pecker would likely bleed to death quickly unless he got to the nearest emergency room.

"Help me," he pleaded, a bloodied hand stretched out, but I ignored him and ran to Devlin.

"Are you okay, did they hurt you?" I asked, carefully scooping her up out of the chair.

"No, I'm okay," she responded softly, before burying her face into my neck.

Little Pecker sat on the floor, in shock, with the knitting needle, still in his eye. "I wouldn't touch that if I were you," I advised.

"Call an... ambulance," Big Pecker gasped.

"Call 'em yourself, Slammer, or better yet, have Flash here run you there really quick," I said before, once again, carrying Devlin out of her apartment.

I got Devlin out to her car, buckled her in, and dialed Minus before taking off for the clinic. I don't know what those animals used to knock Devlin out, but I wanted to make sure she was okay.

"Minus. We've got trouble at Devlin's apartment."

"What kind of trouble?" Minus sounded like he was in no mood at all to hear these words, and I couldn't blame him.

"There was a Spider infestation, and we have some clean-up work to do," I replied.

"Jesus fucking Christ," he replied, and I fought the urge to ask him not to blaspheme. "Were they exterminated?"

"No but wounded pretty badly. We're gonna need a clean-up crew, and they're gonna need an ambulance, pronto. I didn't want to call 9-1-1 and bring the heat, but they're still in her fucking apartment."

"I'll take care of it. You get back to the Sanctuary, now."

"I'm gonna take Devlin to the clinic, and then I'll be right there," I replied, and hung up.

Devlin moaned as I took a sharp turn. "Are you okay? Did they hurt you?"

"I stabbed that man in the eye," she said, calmly.

"Yes, you did, baby. Are you okay?"

"I keep a pair of knitting needles and a bag of yarn tucked under the cushion of that chair," she muttered.

"That was good thinking," I said.

"I... stabbed him." Devlin's voice weakened, and I was afraid she'd pass out again. I hauled ass, taking every side street and short cut I knew on the way to Eldie's.

* * *

Devlin

"Seven staples in my head, and two busted ribs," I heard Ropes report to whoever was on the other end of the line. "Devlin's fine. Eldie's got some fluids in her and wants to watch her for a few hours. I've got Sweet Pea here standing guard while she's here and I'm heading over to the Sanctuary now."

Ropes breached the exam area curtain and smiled wide when he saw me.

"How come you guys never say goodbye?" I asked.

"What baby?"

"The Saints never say goodbye to each other."

"Tradition, I guess. We think it's bad luck to say goodbye to a fellow brother."

"Sounds more like superstition."

"You're probably right." He smiled and squeezed my hand before kissing my forehead.

"How are you feeling?"

"Better."

"Do you remember what happened?" he asked.

"I remember answering the door thinking it was you, and those two bikers were there. I think they knocked me out with chloroform."

"You won't have to worry about them again," I said.

"Aren't those guys with the Saints? I've seen them with you at the bar."

"They used to be recruits in our club, but some shit's gone down and they're now running with the Spiders, a piece of shit club out of Gresham."

"Why?"

"My ex-road captain Wolf is behind all of it. He's pulled off some sort of Lucifer move and dragged a handful of Saints away with him to Hell. Worse than Hell actually, Gresham. Big Pecker and Little Pecker, as we called them, ran with my crew under Wolf. Now Wolf has taken the head seat at the Spiders' table, and he's taken a few of the Saints, including the Peckers with him."

"But what does that all have to do with me? Why did they come to my place?"

"To get to me. Wolf hates my guts because I've always sided with Minus. He probably gave the okay to come after me, and I'm sure Big Pecker jumped at the chance."

"Why?"

"I found out he was spying on us, for Wolf I suppose, so I knocked his front teeth out."

"What is it with you and teeth?"

Ropes shrugged. "Those shitheads are in a lot worse shape now, I'll tell you that."

"What will happen to them now?"

"I called Minus. He'll send someone to get them out of there and clean up your apartment. I'm going to take you back with me to the Sanctuary once Eldie clears you to go."

"This is exactly what you were talking about isn't it? About not wanting to drag me into your crazy life."

Ropes bent down and kissed me softly. "Yes, baby. I'm so sorry."

"You have nothing to be sorry about," I said. "You tried to warn me, and I didn't want to listen. You've never tried to hide who you are from me. I've asked for honesty and you've given me nothing but the truth since day one. I was the one who fucked everything up."

"What are you talking about? You haven't fucked any-thing up. I still feel the same way about you that I always have. That's what I was coming to your apartment to tell you. Nothing's changed for me, Devlin."

"Everything's changed for me!" I yelled, and Ropes took a few steps backward. "I had a plan. It was in writing and everything. I was going to work my ass off as a waitress, save money, tattoo whenever and wherever I could, and open my own shop as soon as possible. Nowhere in this plan was it written, 'fall in love with a fucking biker slash romance novelist slash amateur dentist.'"

"Devlin, I—"

"I'm not finished, so shut your dumb, beautiful mouth,

and don't try to corner me with your words." Ropes wisely said nothing. "Nothing about you, or this crazy fucking life you live fits in with my plan in the least, but here I am, nonetheless. I'm right here, and I'm not going anywhere. Even though you've thrown my entire world off its axis, I'm staying by your side because I love you. I love you and I'll stab a thousand bikers through the eye as long as you say that you love me."

"Can I talk now?"

"Yes, please."

"Never mind. I don't want to," Ropes said and lunged for the bed, kissing me as deeply and passionately as I could ever imagine being kissed.

My hand went to the back of his head, and he winced in pain. "Ow, my staples, baby."

"I'm sorry," I hissed, before returning to our kiss. "Call me baby again."

TWENTY-THREE

BURNING SAINTS

Ropes

TONIGHT WAS THE *night. Max had promised me six hours of uninterrupted time and I'd taken an exorbitant amount of time to get my body ready for him.*

Smoothing the skirt of my dark green dress, I turned sideways in the mirror to make sure everything was perfect and smiled. I could feel the anal beads rubbing deliciously inside of me and I'd had to take several deep breaths to keep myself from orgasming. I'd even had to put on a pair of panties to keep my wetness contained.

My doorbell pealed and I shimmied out of my underwear, sliding into my stilettos before heading to answer Max's summons. I checked the peephole, then pulled open the door and bit my lip as Max's eyes raked over my body. "Well done, Cherry."

I smiled. "Thank you, sir."

"What surprise do you have in store for me?" he asked, stepping inside and closing the door behind him.

I swallowed, leaning down to grasp my ankles and he accepted my invitation to explore, sliding my skirt up my hips.

"Well, well, well," he breathed out, and tugged the beads from my ass.

I shuddered as an orgasm flooded me, unable to stop my body's reaction to his touch.

"I don't remember giving you permission to come," he admonished as his fingers slid through my folds and then his palm slapped my pussy, the sting almost bringing me to climax again.

"I'm sorry, sir."

"Stand up."

I stood up straight and found my dress roughly pulled from my body, leaving me naked and standing on shaky legs.

"You'll keep the shoes on," he directed, and I nodded as he turned me to face him. "You look beautiful."

"Thank you. So do you."

He cupped my breasts, rolling my nipples into tight pebbles. "Tonight I'm going to let you suck me off."

My heart raced and I breathed out, "Thank you, sir."

"First, I want clamps on your tits and your pussy."

I bobbed my head up and down. "They're ready."

"Excellent. Lead the way."

I literally made a run for my bedroom, unable to hide my excitement of getting to wrap my lips around his cock. He let me have him once a week, and since it had already happened this week, I was sure I would have to wait. But he apparently liked what I'd done for him, and that excited me to new levels.

I'd laid out a few of his favorite toys on the bed and I stood with my hands clasped behind me as he perused my choices. Snagging the nipple/clit clamp off the duvet, he smiled down at me. "Spread, Cherry."

I spread, keeping my hands behind me like he preferred and he secured the clamps to my nipples and clit, tightening them to an almost painful point.

Just the way I liked it.

He cupped my mound, putting pressure on the clamp at my clit. "Good?"

"Yes," I hissed out.

He smiled, reaching to unbutton his shirt. I felt my breath hitch as he stripped in front of me, his perfect body on display while the pressure from the clamps almost made me come.

"You may kneel," he said, and I did so immediately.

"Tonight, nothing will be between us."

I gasped. "Really?"

"Yes. You've been asking for this. Have you changed your mind?"

"No," I rushed to say. "Thank you, sir."

"Carry on, Cherry."

I wrapped my hand around his shaft, sliding my mouth down his cock, taking him as deep as I could. My eyes watered with the effort, but I took him deeper and deeper.

Max let me have almost five minutes of cock time before he ordered me to stop.

"Did I do something wrong?"

"No, baby. I want you on your feet."

He helped me stand, then removed my shoes, turning me to face the bed and bending me over the mattress. "Tonight we play."

He took the lube from the nightstand and then stood behind me, running the tip of his cock through my already soaked folds. I heard the click of the tube lid and then cold on my asshole as he worked a finger inside of me. "Okay?"

"Yes," I breathed out.

He pressed the tip of his dick to my entrance and pushed in as I contracted to take him deeper.

"Fuck," he rasped. "So fucking tight."

"Mmm. So good."

He pushed in deeper, then slapped the inside of my thighs

so I'd spread more, before sliding a vibrator into my pussy, pushing me to the brink. "Max," I said on a whimper.

He moved, slowly at first, matching the motion of the vibrator with the motion of his dick, reaching around my body to tug on the chain and I cried out as an orgasm threatened to spill.

"Hold it," he demanded, and slammed into me harder.

"I can't!" I cried out.

"Fucking hold it, Cherry."

"Max, please!"

He pulled out of my ass and I felt the warmth of his cum cover my ass just as I exploded around the vibrator. I had never experienced anything like it and I knew it was why I would never give him up. He was my drug and I was addicted.

Max slid the vibrator out of me and threw it on the bed. "Stay there," he said, and walked to the bathroom, returning with a washcloth to wipe his seed off of me.

Once I was clean, he turned me to sit on the edge of the bed while he wiped his dick until it was hard again. I was always amazed how quickly he could recover from an orgasm. Totally unlike any other man I'd fucked.

"What do you want, Cherry?"

"I want more of your dick in me."

"Where?"

"Oh, god, Max. My ass, please. But I want you to come inside of me."

He grinned slowly and nodded, pushing me onto my back and grabbing the lube again. Slathering it up and down his shaft, he lifted my legs, tugging me to the edge of the bed and slid into me. This gave me some power and I hooked my legs around him to pull him deeper inside me. Picking up the vibrator again, he slipped it into my pussy and turned it on high. I moaned as the vibration connected with the clamp at my clit and resonated to my nipples.

Adjusting the toy so it would stay put, he grasped my thighs and thrust into my asshole deeper. I cried out in ecstasy as he slammed into me repeatedly, the vibrator work-

ing my pussy and the clamps, while his dick made my ass feel like he belonged there.

I screamed his name as I came, my walls contracting around him while he continued to fuck me hard. His quiet grunt was the only indication that he was ready to come and I felt his dick pulse inside of me.

Ungloved as he'd promised.

As he gently pulled out of me, I knew he was mine forever and I smiled as he leaned down and kissed me.

"You ready?" Sweet Pea asked, and I closed my laptop lid.

"Yup, let's go," I said before stuffing the laptop in my bag and stowing it under my bed. I grabbed the backpack sitting on top of my dresser, closed my bedroom door, and followed the others outside.

"Who's got the guest of honor?" I asked my brother.

"I assigned El Presidente to Doozer," he answered.

"Alright," Minus said, addressing the crowd. "Everyone knows the plan, and not to deviate from it. This will only work if we stick together, so absolutely no cowboy shit." Minus turned to Clutch, signaling his turn to address the troops.

"Everyone assigned to carry fire knows what to do with it." Clutch yelled over the crowd. "Get your gun from Ropes and wait for my signal, and my signal alone. Like Minus said, timing is critical, so don't fuck up. Stick with your Road Captains and keep your cool."

"Okay, Saints. Mount the fuck up!" Minus roared, and soon every bike in the Burning Saints Portland Chapter did as well. Days of planning and preparation went into this moment and I'd be lying if I didn't say it was as exciting as it was terrifying.

We rode together in a great mass of leather and chrome, pipes blaring at a deafening volume through the streets of Portland. The shockwave of our convoy set off several car alarms parked along the city streets. We hit the highway and headed east toward Gresham, straight into the Spiders' web, where the others were already in position.

Gresham is a semi-rural, working class city, nestled between Portland and the foothills of the Cascade Mountains. The Spiders' clubhouse is in a remote area, just south of the city. Unlike Portland and Seattle, which contained several clubs that co-existed more-or-less peacefully over the years, Gresham had always been ruled by one club alone, the Spiders. This was due mostly to the ever-growing meth trade in their city, and the Spiders' dominance in the market. The Spiders' founder, Char, was a brutal and ruthless leader, and his current prison term didn't appear to be slowing down his or his club's progress. In fact, now that Char was inside, he appeared to have gained contacts and street level intel. The Gresham Spiders had goals to become simply The Spiders, a nation-wide gang of one-percent bikers, and they were on the fast track to do so.

According to Kitty's intel, Char reached out to Wolf when he heard about his dissatisfaction with the Saints' new direction. Apparently, Wolf was shooting his mouth off at a card game that was also attended by a few members of the Spiders. Who knows, maybe Wolf knew they were there and wanted them to hear him. Either way, word got back to Char, who then approached him about running the Portland chapter. Due to internal club issues, he didn't have a trustworthy next in line and thought Wolf might just be his kind of asshole. Apparently, Char was right, and Wolf wasted no time secretly recruiting disgruntled Saints to go with him. Wolf was clearly smart about his choices, as no one he approached said anything to Minus or turned him down. No one until my brother that is.

I asked Sweet Pea what Wolf said to him to make him knock him on his ass, and he just shrugged and said Wolf asked him to come with him and the punch was his answer. I knew my brother well enough to know his answer was horseshit, but I also knew him enough not to press for further details. Either way, I felt bad for even having a shred of doubt about my brother's loyalty to the club or to Minus. Still, this had to be tearing him up. Wolf, more than anyone in the club, was like a father to Sweet Pea and there had to be a part of him that wanted to go with him, especially since I know that he often disagrees with Minus. But in the end, Sweet Pea would never turn his back on me or his club brothers, and he'd clearly proved it by putting hands on a club president. Even if Wolf was some sort of puppet leader for the Spiders. The code was the code, and there were certain things a biker just didn't do. Hitting a President was one of them, and I knew he'd have a target on his back so long as the Spiders were an active club.

TWENTY-
FOUR

BURNING SAINTS

Ropes

WE REACHED THE road leading to the Spiders' clubhouse just after midnight. Killing our engines and lights, we rolled our bikes to the outer perimeter of their place, and approached the two-story, farmhouse quietly. The house was located on several acres of farmland, surrounded by a crescent-shaped ridge caused by volcanic activity from nearby Mt. Hood, a non-dormant volcano and ski resort. People call our lifestyle crazy and meanwhile motherfuckers ski down a volcano and no one bats an eyelash. The ridge surrounded the property, giving the Spiders ultimate privacy to do whatever the fuck they wanted out here. It was dark, desolate, creepy as fuck, and matched the dark mystique the club had built around itself over the years.

"This is far enough," Minus whispered, and our group came to a halt and parked our bikes in the tall grass.

"You sure they're all home, Prez?" Warthog asked.

"They've gotta go to church just like everyone else," Minus replied. "This is when and where they do it."

"Why at midnight?" Warthog asked.

"Probably some sort of 'We're evil, black cat, voo-doo bullshit,'" Minus replied. "Okay, time to go bust up a tea party," he said and walked toward the farmhouse. His steps were slow and careful. It was dark as hell out here, and if not for the light of a nearly full moon, he wouldn't be able to see two steps ahead of him. Who knows what kind of booby traps the Spiders may have set out here.

From where we were positioned, we could clearly see the farmhouse as most of the inside lights were on. We could hear music and raised voices cutting through the otherwise quiet night. Minus continued to creep forward in the darkness until a spotlight flooded directly down on him. He froze in place and calmly put his hands in the air.

"Who the fuck are you?" A raspy voice called out from what sounded like a rear, second story window.

"Minus, from the Burning Saints. I came to talk to Wolf," he shouted back.

"What are you doing here, Minus?"

"I've got business."

"I doubt you've got any business being here tonight."

"Look, I know Wolf is in there. I'm unarmed, and I just want to talk. He's gonna want to hear what I have to say, believe me."

The spotlight tuned off with a loud clank and a row of soft lights came up on the back porch, revealing Wolf, and what appeared to be his new officers standing in a row. From what I could make out, his cabinet was a mixture of longtime Spiders and some of those that had defected from the Saints. I wanted to break the line and tear Wolf's throat out myself but stowed that shit immediately.

"Minus, I've always known you to be a man that respected tradition," Wolf bellowed. "So, it surprises the holy, living fuck outta me that you'd show up uninvited, during church."

"Sounds more like a party than church."

"Maybe you haven't heard, the Spiders are patching in their new Portland Chapter President tonight," Wolf said, his arms stretched out.

"I guess my invitation got lost in the mail." Minus mocked a smile and slowly lowered his hands.

"Must be it. I'll tell the boys you dropped by. Most of them are inside, including one youngster with an eyepatch that would love some time alone with your boy Ropes."

"The Peckers came at him and his old lady," Minus replied. "They defended themselves."

"*The Peckers* are now named Slammer and Flash and are full-patch members of the Spiders, and your boy is gonna pay."

"Congratulations to them," Minus said dryly.

"Slammer nearly died from a knife wound, and Flash lost an eye. You think we're gonna let that slide?"

"Like I said, your boys came after Ropes, so the way I see it, our clubs are even on that."

"Well that ain't the way we see it."

Minus shrugged. "It's probably not the way Flash sees it either, with the one eye and all."

The tension of the moment squashed my urge to laugh at what was some grade A shit talk from Minus.

"Keep making jokes now, Minus. You won't be laughing when we're mailing you Ropes's fingers, the way he mails teeth. Flash has a pair of pruning shears and a plan for which finger he removes on which day of the week."

I grit my teeth and used every ounce of self-control I had to not call out to Flash and Wolf to come at me right then and there.

"I'll be sure to tell him," Minus said, calmly.

"You do that," Wolf replied. "You be sure to tell that brother of his I'm gonna personally do a lot worse to him next time we cross paths."

"Look, Wolf. I'm not here to start shit, I'm here to end it.

I'm here to talk business."

"What the fuck kind of business could I possibly have with you?"

"The business of staying in business," Minus replied. "Word is out about Char's plans to deal in Portland and Seattle and I'm here to advise you to ditch that plan."

By now, some of the other Spiders' members had joined their brothers on the porch. Wolf dialed up his bravado. "You think you get to dictate the way money flows around here? I don't think you quite understand the current balance of power, Minus. The Spiders already own Gresham, and with you and the Saints gone, we'll take over all of Portland soon enough. We're gonna push north through Seattle and we ain't gonna stop until we hit ice, motherfucker. Shit, I'll put Spiders patches on dudes with snowmobiles and dog sleds if I want."

The Spiders cheered in support of their new chapter President.

"The entire Northwest, huh?" Minus asked.

"Who's gonna fucking stop me? The Burning Saints? You're out of the blood business Minus. You've been banging that drum like Jack fucking Henry for everyone in town to hear."

"That doesn't mean I'm gonna roll over and let you take Portland. The Burning Saints are always going to ride in our hometown. Just because we're not earning by the sword doesn't mean I won't spill blood, mine or yours. I'll do whatever it takes to protect my club. Make no mistake about that."

"Or, I could just kill you right here and now," Wolf spat out.

My hand gripped my pistol. I wanted so badly to fire right at the head of that traitorous bastard but reminded myself again to stick to the plan.

Wolf continued, "The same guy that had that spotlight on you earlier, has a bead on your cranium with a high-powered rifle. He's equipped with a night vision scope and did four tours as an Army sniper. All I have to do is give the signal and you're dead before you hit the ground."

"I wouldn't do that if I were you," Minus replied.

"Why the fuck not?" Wolf challenged.

Minus let out two short whistles and those of us that rode in with Minus hit our headlights, revealing his ground support, but shielding our identities.

"It looks like even more people came to my party," Wolf howled. "Well, don't I feel fuckin' special? Nice turnout, but it still doesn't explain why I shouldn't just waste you right here and now. I count a few headlights, but we still outnumber your asses big-time."

"Well, you see," Minus drawled. "That's what I wanted to talk to you about." He let out two more whistles, and those of us that were armed, fired our flare guns into the air simultaneously. Seconds later, the night sky was illuminated by a bright red flash, which revealed the silhouette of around seventy-five armed bikers positioned on the ridgeline above the property.

"The Burning Saints alone may not have the numbers or the fire power to take you on, but together we all do," Minus said, motioning to the mass of bikers that loomed over their clubhouse. "Unlike the Spiders, the Saints have tried to build bridges and mend fences with other local clubs over the years. The Dogs of Fire in Portland and the Primal Howlers in Colorado are standing with us to send you a message."

"What message would that be?" Wolf sneered.

"The Spiders need to back down."

"Or what?" Wolf laughed. "Even with the Dogs and the Primal Howlers backing you, you still don't have enough firepower or manpower to stop the Spiders."

"That's where he comes in," Minus motioned behind him, and an elderly Mexican man, dressed in white, stepped out of the darkness.

The gathering of Spiders muttered among themselves, clearly surprised to see the founder of Los Psychos standing with Minus. The infamous Mexican club had recently been at war with the Burning Saints, but Minus had brokered a peace treaty dependent on a fair handoff of the protection rackets from our club to theirs. No one expected the peace to last, as Los Psychos were notorious on both sides of the border as being as brutal as an MC could be.

"You know El Cacto," Minus said. "And you know that he and I have a deal, the protection business in Portland belongs to him now."

"That was your deal, not the Spiders'," Wolf shouted back.

"That makes no difference to Los Psychos. Interfere with my business and you'll deal with my soldiers," El Cacto said. Minus gave his final signal, launching a second volley of flares into the sky.

This time, over a hundred members of Los Psychos came riding in from the outer darkness, pipes blaring, signaling everyone on the ridge to ride down and join Minus with the rest of the Burning Saints. All together, we were over two hundred strong. Most of us armed, all of us ready for a reason to end Wolf right then and there. Once everyone had reached the bottom of the basin, we killed our engines, and a cloud of dust passed over El Cacto and Minus as he called out to Wolf once again.

"This is your last warning. Stay out of Portland, and you tell Char that his plans for expansion have been cancelled. You and the Spiders have broken the code, and the code still stands for something."

"What the fuck do you know about the code? What do you know about loyalty? You're the one that's gonna get your whole fuckin' club killed. Mark my words, boy. You ain't warning me, I'm warning you."

"So, you're choosing war?" Minus asked.

"I'm saying I'll talk to Char about this and whatever he says, stands. If he says strap up, then so be it, but if he says make the peace then maybe I'll only cripple you instead of kill you."

"You are playing a dangerous game my friend," El Cacto said.

"Unlike your new amigo there, I don't play around, old man. I'll stand down for now and let you all ride the fuck outta here in one piece, but I can assure you this ain't over."

"No, it's not. The Spiders' meth trade has flourished in Gresham only because Los Psychos have allowed it. We've kept an eye on your club over the years, and you've always stayed within your bounds, but now Char is getting greedy, so Los Psychos needs to rethink our position on your club."

"You do all the thinking you want, old man. It doesn't mean we have to do what you say," Wolf said to El Cacto before turning and pointing at Minus, "And you'd better watch your back."

"You're not just picking a fight with our club anymore, Wolf. You're starting a war."

"It wasn't me that brought these people onto our land. You dragged these clubs into your fight because you're not man enough to handle shit on your own."

"Char drew first blood when he poached you from the Saints."

"Poached me?" Wolf laughed. "Who the fuck told you Char poached me. I came to the Spiders because I wanted to ride with a real club again. I want to drink Jager, eat pussy and make real fucking money again. A bunch of your club members feel the same way, they're just too chicken shit to say so. The ones that weren't scared, the smart ones, came with me."

"There's nothing smart about this play, Wolf," Minus said.

"I guess we'll see, won't we? Now, you go ahead and join the rest of the Justice League and ride on out of here. I'll talk to Char and get back to you with our answer about halting our expansion plans, but stick around here any longer, and I don't care how many of you there are, shots are gonna start flying."

"You know where to find me," Minus said, and joined us before leading our convoy back to the highway.

Devlin

T HE SOUND OF motorcycles approaching made my heart race. I was still completely terrified of those death machines, but now when I heard pipes I thought of Ropes, and when I thought of Ropes, my body reacted. Ropes and some of the other officers had been gone all day on club business and I hadn't been able to reach him. I'd texted, but no response, which was totally unlike him.

A physical reaction at the mere thought of a man was something entirely new to me. I'd heard being in love described as butterflies in the stomach but thinking about Ropes gave me a feeling more akin to a swarm of bees whose hive had just been disturbed. Being with Ropes meant constantly walking an emotional tightrope between feeling completely safe, and utterly terrified.

On one hand, I knew that, together, he and I could face any challenge. On the other, I knew there would be a lot of challenges to come. This was already evident by the fact that I'd been staying in Ropes's cramped bedroom for the better part of a week, hiding out like some sort of fugitive while he, Minus, and the others were preparing for a turf war.

I heard several bikes pull in through the security gate and park. I stood up and checked myself in the dresser mirror. I was wearing a new bra that looked great, but didn't quite fit right. Ropes loved my tits, so I always made sure they were perfectly on display. Truth be told, I felt my sexiest when the girls were out to play. As I cupped my left breast to make the needed adjustment, my fingernail grazed my nipple, sending shivers up my spine. I paused for a moment before repeating the motion, this time increasing the pressure of my nail against the sensitive skin. I let out a quiet gasp and my left hand slid underneath my jeans, between my thighs. I knew Ropes would be walking through the door at any moment, but the pressure of my hand felt amazing against my wet pussy. I pinched my nipple harder and widened my stance as I fingered my swollen clit, my breathing now reduced to short gasps. I increased both the speed and pressure of my movements as I envisioned Ropes walking in on me and finishing the job. I was ready to feel his beard against my inner thighs. Ready for his tongue to replace my fingers. But more than anything I was ready for him to…

A knock at the bedroom door broke my rhythm. And I huffed sexual frustration before calling out, "Come in." I had spontaneously worked myself into a tizzy and needed Ropes to fuck me, immediately.

"You wanna give me a hand?" I asked playfully, turning to see Cricket, Minus's old lady and club business manager standing in the doorway. She was dressed in a charcoal grey suit jacket and skirt. I, on the other hand, was in jeans, a t-shirt, and two knuckles deep into my flower pot.

"Jebus!" I screamed, frantically stuffing lady lefty back into the ill-fitting garment that started all of this.

"Should I come back another time?" Cricket asked, smiling.

"No," I said, completely mortified. "I was just… getting dressed. I… I thought you were Ropes."

"Clearly," she replied with a wink.

"I'm so embarrassed," I said, just as Ropes arrived.

"Hey, Cricket," Ropes greeted her with a kiss on the cheek. "What are you embarrassed about baby?"

"I—"

Cricket jumped in before I made an even bigger fool of myself. "Devlin just needed to borrow something from me. Lady stuff. No concern of yours."

"Say no more," Ropes said, throwing his hands in the air.

"Speaking of borrowing," Cricket continued. "May I borrow Devlin for a bit?"

My head snapped to Cricket. "Me?"

"Just for a few minutes, if you have the time," Cricket replied cheerily.

"Sure, of course," I said, unable to fathom what Cricket needed to talk to me about.

Ropes leaned in for a quick kiss. "We'll catch up when you're done with Cricket. I'm gonna take a shower and get dressed, and then we can go out to eat. Sound good?"

"Sounds great," I said before turning to Cricket. "I'm just gonna go freshen up really quickly."

"I'll be in Minus's office. Just come find me whenever you're ready," Cricket said and disappeared down the hall.

After cleaning up and changing into a bra that fit, I stopped off in the kitchen before heading to Minus's office. I didn't know what Cricket wanted to talk to me about but based on the little information Ropes could share with me, and the mood around the clubhouse, it was bound to be something bad. The best I could figure was Cricket had been set with the task of kicking me out of the Sanctuary. Minus probably gave her the job because it would be easier to hear it from another woman. I'd probably pissed Minus off or broken some cardinal rule while staying here, maybe even just me being here was a violation. Of course, it could be worse. Maybe Ropes wanted me gone and this was how you broke up with someone in club culture.

If I was walking into an ambush or a firing squad, I wanted a drink first. I raided Warthog's infamous liquor cabinet, and the fridge until I found what I needed to make a passable Captain Blue Breeze. For just a moment, I was transported back to the boat, to a simpler time when life made just a little more sense. A time before I lived in a biker's bedroom or was caught in the middle of a gang war. A time before I was given to fits of public masturbation or drinking before six P.M.

I finished the drink, put the glass in the sink, and made my way to the office of the Burning Saints President, where I was sure to face my demise.

I found the office door open and gave it a couple of gentle raps as I poked my head inside. "Hi, Devlin," Cricket said cheerily, from behind Minus's desk. "Thank you for making the time for me."

"Of course," I said. "Any time."

"You've been the topic of several conversations between me and Minus as of late, so I thought it was time I start talking *to* you instead of *about* you."

I swallowed and braced myself for the worst.

"Minus and I think you are amazing and would like to invest in a tattoo shop with you. Much like our deal with Sally Anne and her bar, the club would be your silent partner and you'd run the place. You'd have the benefit of the Club's protection, and in return, our guys get an employee discount on any ink. We split the profit 80/20 with you getting the bigger piece. What do you think?"

I burst into tears. "I have no idea what to say, I'm in shock."

I couldn't believe that in a few seconds, I'd leapt so much farther ahead to realizing my biggest goal.

"Take all the time you need to think about it," Cricket said.

"All the time I need is right now. Are you kidding? My answer is yes."

"Good. I'm excited to hear that, and I know Minus will be as well. We have a lot of faith that this will be a successful business venture for both you and the club."

"What about Ropes?"

"What do you mean?" Cricket asked.

"I guess I mean, what if he and I don't end up being quite such a successful venture? Couldn't that complicate things?"

"Perhaps, but we're all adults here. Besides, if Ropes dumps you, or does anything stupid to screw up what the two of you have, I'll personally make sure he needs more staples in his head."

With my heart full, I hugged Cricket, then made my way back to Ropes's room. Virtually throwing myself into his arms, I kissed him. "Thank you, thank you, thank you," I said between kisses.

"The tattoo shop was Cricket's idea," he said. "But I'll take the kisses."

"I know you had something to do with it."

"I can neither confirm nor deny those allegations. Either way, it really was Cricket's idea, and I think both the idea and you are amazing."

"Thanks babe, I'm so excited."

"Me too." He smiled. "Love you."

"I love you too."

"How about I take you out for a celebratory dinner?"

"How about you eat me out instead?"

He chuckled and began his work where I left off.

His love had been a surprise and I planned to treasure it forever.

Devlin

One year later...

I STOOD AT the altar and grinned at my New York Times Bestselling Author groom. Father Finn had just pronounced us man and wife and declared, "You may make the deal."

Ropes shoved his hand out and I slid mine in it and squeezed as we shook on our marriage. It was how he proposed.

"A handshake is a deal that can't be broken," he'd said from bended knee. He'd opened a red jewelry box to reveal a ring with a two-carat pear-shaped diamond, nestled in a halo of smaller diamonds, and asked me to marry him. I'd im-

mediately said yes, but he held his hand out to me anyway. "Make the deal."

I took his hand and shook it, then threw myself into his arms, both of us falling onto the deck of the ship. We were on the Books and Booze Cruise again and he'd waited until everyone was on deck to propose.

Olivia and Ali opened bottles of champagne, spraying us until we were soaked, and then we partied until the wee hours of the morning.

Now they sat in the front row ready to pop more bubbly, while Darien and Cricket stood as my bridesmaids. Once we shook hands, Ropes pulled me into his arms and kissed me, dipping me low to the hoots and hollers of his club. He was careful not to crush my veil, but I held him tightly just in case he dropped me.

Breaking the kiss, he grinned down at me and put me back on my feet. "I love you."

I smiled slowly. "I love you, too."

"I present to you Mr. and Mrs. Kimble," Father Finn said. "Let's party!"

And we did.

Until the next day.

Things were still uncertain in the biker world, but in my world, things were perfect. I was in love, the tattoo shop was booming, and Ropes was getting the recognition he so greatly deserved.

We'd just closed on a gorgeous little house in Vancouver, close to a few of the Dogs of Fire crew. In fact, the Sergeant at Arms, Hatch, had a sweet hookup in the form of his brother who owned a construction company. His name was Cullen and he was going to update our house while we were on our honeymoon.

Ropes and I both had complete faith in him, but he'd promised he'd send pictures and keep us updated as things progressed.

For now, though, it was time to celebrate our wedding and as I watched my husband dance with Cricket, I felt the blessing of him deep in my soul.

I smiled as I thought of a future with him, standing side by side, growing old together. Because, after all, a deal's a deal.

)!

1 fluid ounce light rum
1 fluid ounce blue Curacao liqueur
1 fluid ounce of orange vodka
2 fluid ounces pineapple juice

Combine rum, blue Curacao, pineapple juice, vodka, and pour over ice.

Garnish with a slice of pineapple and a maraschino cherry.

USA Today Bestselling Author Jack Davenport is a true romantic at heart, but he has a rebel's soul. His writing is passionate, energetic, and often fueled by his true life, fiery romance with author wife, Piper Davenport.

Twenty-five years as a professional musician lends a unique perspective into the world of rock stars, while his outlaw upbringing gives an authenticity to his MC series.

Like Jack's FB page and get to know him!
(www.facebook.com/jackdavenportauthor)

Made in the USA
Monee, IL
18 February 2023

28193040R00128